THE KILLING GAME

"Feel that?" came Lee's voice from the blackness of the tunnel.

A current of cool, salty air curled around Rebecca's feet. She felt Lee's hand grope for hers. He pulled her along until the tunnel got wider and they saw four bright cracks of yellow, the outline of a doorway.

They crept up to it. They heard muffled voices from behind the door.

"I told you to stay out of sight!" It was Fletcher's voice.

"I did!" The voice that answered spoke with an accent. "It was so hot in this little room that I *had* to go out for air . . ."

"Stay away from their camp. In fact, don't go anywhere near them!" Fletcher yelled. "They're suspicious enough as it is. Especially Rebecca and Lee. I can see it in their eyes. They've already found my weapons room. I found one of my arrows stuck in the front door of the house this morning."

"I'm sorry, Eduardo."

"I want everything to go off without a hitch tomorrow." Fletcher said. "I brought you here to do a job, not to go sightseeing. Keep your nocturnal wanderings to the vicinity of the north cliffs, Jorge."

"*Sí*, Eduardo."

"Until the killing game is over."

YOU WON'T BE SCARED ... *NOT* AND YOU'LL *SCREAM* FOR MORE!
Bone-chilling horror from Z-FAVE

SCREAM #1: BLOOD PACT (4355, $3.50)
Jamie Fox and her friends decide to fake a "suicide" pact when they find out their hang out, an old train depot, is going to be demolished. They sign their names in blood, but of course, never really intend to kill themselves.

Now, one by one, the signers of the pact begin to die in what looks like suicide. But Jamie suspects murder, and will be the next to die ... unless she can unmask the cunning killer who's watching her every move!

SCREAM #2: DEADLY DELIVERY (4356, $3.50)
Derek Cliver and his friends have recently joined The Terror Club, an exciting new mail-order club, which allows them the fantasy of "disposing" of those that they despise with monsters of their own creation. But now the game is terrifyingly real because these monsters have come to life—and are actually killing.

The body count is rising as Derek and his friends somehow must undo what they've done ... before they become the next victims!

SCREAM #3: WANTED TO RENT (4357, $3.50)
Sixteen-year-old Christy Baker is really worried. There is something about her family's handsome boarder that gives her the creeps. Things get even creepier when she finds a length of rope, masking tape, newspaper clippings about murdered women ... and a photo of herself ... in his room.

Now Christy is home alone. The downstairs door has just opened. She knows who's come in—and why he's there!

Available wherever paperbacks are sold, or order direct from the Publisher. Send cover price plus 50¢ per copy for mailing and handling to Penguin USA, P.O. Box 999, c/o Dept. 17109, Bergenfield, NJ 07621. Residents of New York and Tennessee must include sales tax. DO NOT SEND CASH.

THE KILLING GAME

Bruce Richards

Z•FAVE
KENSINGTON PUBLISHING CORP.

Z*FAVE BOOKS are published by

Kensington Publishing Corp.
850 Third Avenue
New York, NY 10022

Copyright © 1994 by Bruce Richards

All rights reserved. No part of this book may be reproduced in any form or by any means without the prior written consent of the Publisher, excepting brief quotes used in reviews.

If you purchased this book without a cover, you should be aware that this book is stolen property. It was reported as "unsold and destroyed" to the Publisher and neither the Author nor the Publisher has received any payment for this "stripped book."

Z*FAVE and the Z*FAVE logo are trademarks of Kensington Publishing Corp.

First Printing: November, 1994

Printed in the United States of America

One

Night was falling by the time Cara Worthington walked into the Night Owl Club, strutting across the floor with the energy of a frenetic bumblebee. The mound of red crimped hair that framed her pretty round face was bobbing and wiggling as she made her way over to where Rebecca Swenson sat in a corner booth, patiently waiting for the bitch goddess to arrive.

Rebecca watched Cara weave her way through the Friday night crowd. She studied Cara's face and braced herself. The familiar green eyes were glowing brightly, the lips had that tight pucker to them, the cheeks a rosy glow, the jaw firm and jutting—the expression Cara usually wore when she was in a foul mood.

She had been waiting for Cara Worthington for over an hour.

She would have waited another hour. And another hour after that. Cara was rich and she was beautiful and she had connections. In other words, she possessed more power than any teenage girl should be allowed to have.

"What a day!" Cara complained as she slid into the booth opposite Rebecca, poking around in her purse. She removed a small gold pill box and popped a Valium into her mouth. She swallowed it dry. "My sweater's ruined!"

"What happened?" asked Rebecca, trying to sound sympathetic, as if she cared what happened to yet another of Cara's expensive possessions.

"Brian's stupid cousin Lee got grease on my brand new Donna Karan cashmere sweater. Now it's ruined! Look!" She thrust out her ample bosom for Rebecca to inspect. Brian was Cara's rich boyfriend.

Rebecca peered dutifully but saw nothing. Upon closer examination, she detected a barely discernible smudge on the breast of the sweater.

"I guess you'll just have to throw it away," Rebecca said, trying to hide her sarcasm.

She envied Cara. She envied Shannen Doherty. In fact, she envied anyone who had a lot of money, having been poor herself all her life. She watched as Cara made the smudge worse by rubbing it with her thumb. The light from a lit candle on the table reflected off one of her diamond rings.

"Maybe the dry cleaner can get it out," Rebecca suggested.

"Forget it," Cara moaned loudly, giving up, inspecting her highly buffed fingernails for any sign of dirt. "You can't get grease out. I should make that jerk pay for it. Except I doubt if he makes enough in a year to pay for a sweater like this."

"How'd it happen?" Rebecca asked, stifling a yawn.

Cara must have over a hundred sweaters in her closet, half of which Rebecca hadn't even seen her wear yet. Cara's closet at home was roughly the same size as their dorm room at the Cooper Riding Academy.

Cara was obviously pleased to have an audience. "The lout was working on Brian's Jag and rubbed up against me. On purpose, I'm sure, the pervert."

Cara started rubbing the smudge again. Rebecca figured it was just a matter of time before she rubbed a hole right through the sweater.

"Then he got all huffy just because I called him a grease monkey—"

Rebecca laughed out loud. She wondered if Cara realized what she was saying half the time.

Cara glared at Rebecca.

"You think it's funny? Do you know how much this sweater cost? Probably more money than your entire wardrobe put together."

Rebecca tried to ignore the put-down. "I'm sure it was an accident," she said quietly.

"I doubt it," Cara persisted. "Brian's usually such a gentleman, but Lee is part Neanderthal. How Brian's aunt could have married an *immigrant*, I'll never know." Cara said "immigrant" like it was a dirty word. Rebecca's grandparents were immigrants from Sweden—but she didn't mention that to Cara, whose family had come to the United States over two hundred years ago.

It had been the luck of the draw that the two girls had ended up roommates at the Cooper Riding Academy, and Rebecca was determined to take advantage of it. Cara was her ticket to the world of rich boys and society functions.

But it wasn't easy to stay friends with Cara. It had taken Rebecca almost the entire school year to adjust to Cara's thin pink skin and fluctuating moods. But it would be worth the effort if only Cara would introduce her to Mr. Right—rich, handsome, Mr. Right. And Cara had introduced her to lots of guys—rich guys, some were even good-looking. But none of them were even close to being Mr. Right, Rebecca lamented. Some of the guys just pawed her throughout their date. Others were cold fishes who shook hands with her when they said good night as if she had just bought some insurance from them. Rebecca had yet to meet a guy she really liked—someone who could make her feel the way Cara said Brian made her feel. In bed.

Cara wasn't shy about telling Rebecca every last detail of her sex life. She knew Rebecca was still a virgin and thought that incredibly old-fashioned. But Rebecca wasn't in a hurry, and there was no way she would climb into bed with a country club jerk just because he was rich. So she waited.

It was Rebecca's idea to meet at the Night Owl to talk about their summer plans—in only two more weeks they would be free for the entire summer. Except freedom for Rebecca, unlike her rich friend, probably meant a summer of drudgery.

"Well, I guess we have more important things to discuss than yet another sweater I look beautiful in," Cara said, now bored with the subject—or perhaps the Valium she popped a few minutes ago had kicked in, Rebecca thought. "I'm thinking of going to Paris for the summer. No—forget about Paris. If I have to look at that stupid Eiffel Tower one more time I think I'll drop from boredom. Have you ever been to Paris?"

"No."

"The Eiffel Tower's nothing but a big erector set. I don't see why they make such a big deal about it . . . maybe I'll go to China. I've never been to Peking—or is it Beijing? Is that in China?"

"I think so, yes."

"Except Chinese food is so fattening. All that sweet and sour pork, yuck," Cara said, scrunching up her face.

Rebecca silently shook her head. There wasn't an ounce of fat on Cara, who had the body of a gymnast, with the exception of her two large breasts. She kept that body in perfect shape with plenty of aerobics classes, body building, jogging, tennis, and sex.

Cara loved to work out. She thrived on it and she was a great all around athlete. As was Rebecca. It was something—maybe the only thing—the girls had in common.

"Forget about China," Cara said.

Maybe the only thing.

Rebecca Swenson pushed a wisp of blond hair away from her tanned, slightly freckled face. Her hair was long and blond, and she usually brushed it straight back over her shoulders or sometimes pulled it into a ponytail or single French braid. She knew she was as pretty as Cara with her lively blue eyes, creamy pale skin, and long tanned legs.

"I don't know why I'm even torturing myself thinking about summer vacation plans," Cara complained. "I may not even go. I got into this incredible argument with my father last night over a few little credit card bills I ran up. I don't know what's up with him but suddenly he's come down with this major attitude. I overheard him tell my mother last night he thought I should get a *job* this summer—"

"A job!" Rebecca exclaimed in mock terror, her eyes wide. "Surely he can't be serious!"

"Something about teaching me responsibility," Cara said with a groan. Caught up in her misery, she wasn't even aware Rebecca was teasing her. "I just don't know what to do. What about you? Have you decided where you're going? The Alps are nice this time of year," she suggested.

"I don't know, yet. I haven't made up my mind." As if I have a choice. I'll probably be slinging burgers at McDonald's or something equally exciting, Rebecca thought. I haven't made up my mind just how I'll bore myself to death this summer. Well, what could she do? She attended the Cooper Riding Academy on a scholarship and *had* to take a summer job to help cover expenses for the coming school year.

"I asked my father if *he* made so much money why *I* had to be responsible? He didn't even bother to answer me. Just gave me a big, blank stare." Cara shook her head sadly. "That man can be so mean and manipulative."

"Of course he's mean and manipulative," Rebecca deadpanned. "He's your father."

Although Rebecca had to admit she was no expert on fathers. Her father had left her mother and her when Rebecca was a baby and they hadn't heard from him since. Her mother worked as a ticket taker at the Plaza Cinema 4 in Cooper Hollow, when she wasn't nipping at her gin bottle in the shadows of her bedroom in their grungy little house.

The pleasant aroma of pizza came wafting toward them from the direction of the snack bar. "What about Italy?" Rebecca suggested.

"Hmmm . . ." Cara murmured. "I haven't been to Rome in years. Except Italian boys are so . . . I don't know . . . oily. Like Brian's cousin—" Cara suddenly steeled herself.

Rebecca glanced over her shoulder and saw Brian McCracken enter the room with an olive-skinned boy she vaguely recognized. Brian looked around, spotted them, and approached their booth with the boy in tow.

"Hi, there," Brian said. Rebecca nodded pleasantly as Cara returned to her funky mood. "Ah . . . Rebecca, I'd like you to meet my cousin Lee. Lee, this is Rebecca, Cara's roommate."

Lee nodded and stretched a greasy hand across the table to shake Rebecca's hand, knocking over her diet soda. The sticky brown liquid slopped all over the sleeve of Cara's brand new Donna Karan cashmere sweater. Lee muttered an apology, reached for a pile of napkins to hand to Cara, and knocked over the sugar dispenser.

"You jackass!" Cara shouted loud enough for everyone in the crowded room to hear. A hush fell over the crowd as all eyes turned toward them.

A scowl formed upon Lee's face. "I said I was sorry!"

Cara grabbed the napkins from Lee's hand and started dabbing at the sticky stuff soaking quickly into the soft fabric of her sweater.

The buzz in the room gradually picked up again.

Brian smiled at Rebecca, displaying his perfect teeth. "You'll have to forgive Lee. He was just released from the

THE KILLING GAME

Juvenile Detention Center and he's not yet acclimated to civilization."

"Thanks, cuz," Lee said flatly. "Why don't you just tattoo a warning on my forehead so everyone will know to get out of my way?"

Brian's bemused smile widened as he continued to apply the needle. "And then his father just lost his job at the post office. Don't worry about it, cuz. I told you, Father will give him a job on the loading dock." Brian's family owned a very profitable trucking company.

Lee glowered in silence.

"I was just telling Lee on the way over here that if his father does well on the loading dock, my father may be able to find something easier for him at the plant. Perhaps on the janitorial staff. I'm sure cleaning the toilets will be less of a strain on his back than lifting all those heavy boxes." Brian was taking a sadistic pleasure in humiliating Lee in front of the two girls.

"My old man can do any job your old man's got for him," Lee shot back.

"I doubt that. Your father's a drunk," Brian countered.

"He's gone on the wagon," Lee asserted.

"Let's be honest, cuz. All alcoholics say that when they're looking for work. They need the money for that next bottle."

"Think so?" Lee asked angrily, a fire burned in his dark-brown, soulful eyes.

"Know so," Brian said smugly.

Lee was about to reply but clammed up instead. A vein poked out on his forehead and Rebecca was caught in the rhythm of it throbbing. She thought for a moment it might explode and spray blood all over Cara's sweater.

Rebecca's eyes wandered over the rest of his face: thick black eyebrows arched over his sad, dark eyes; a slightly hooked nose; chiseled jaw; thick curly black hair. Then her gaze strayed down to his biceps which bulged from beneath a very dirty, very greasy T-shirt.

His tough guy image was only slightly interrupted by the diamond stud earring that glittered from one of his ears. Suddenly, Lee excused himself and left the table in stony silence.

Rebecca watched him go. From behind he was built like a capital "T," with square broad shoulders tapering down to a thin, almost girlish waist.

"I wonder where he's going in such a hurry?" Brian said to no one in particular.

Rebecca turned toward Brian. "I think you may have hurt his feelings."

Brian laughed it off. "Oh, he'll get over it. I doubt much can penetrate that thick skull of his."

"I don't know," Rebecca said. "He looks like he has a quick trigger. I don't think I'd push him too far."

"Oh . . ." Brian said, dismissing her warning with a wave of his hand. "That's nothing compared to Cara's temper."

Suddenly Rebecca remembered where she had seen Lee before. It was her sophomore year at Cooper Hollow High, before she transferred to the riding academy. Lee Spaghetti— or something like that.

He was only a junior at the time, and already Cooper Hollow High's star fullback. Part bulldozer, part deer, he was a tough runner to bring down, if you could catch him.

"Sorry I had to bring him along," Brian apologized to Cara. "Lee got kicked out of school and now I have to drag him around with me everywhere. To keep him out of trouble. Daddy's orders. Lee's mother made Father promise to keep an eye on the boy before she died of cancer." Brian made it sound as if his aunt had died specifically to make his own life more difficult. "Naturally, Father shuffles him off onto me."

THE KILLING GAME

"Why?" Rebecca asked. "I mean, why did Lee get kicked out of school?"

"Joy riding in a stolen car. Father assumes his delinquent friends talked him into it, so I'm supposed to make certain he steers clear of them." Brian groaned, then resumed his martyr demeanor. "What a pain it is being a babysitter all the time." He looked across the table at Rebecca, a glimmer of embarrassment in his eyes. Rebecca babysat every chance she could to earn some extra pocket money. "So . . . what do you think of my heathen cousin?"

"What time do you return him to his cage?" Cara answered for her.

Brian nudged Cara in the ribs with his elbow. "Not you. I know what you think."

Rebecca shot a nervous glance in Cara's direction. "Actually, I think he's kind of cute . . ."

Cara was looking at her with a horrified expression on her face. "You can't be serious. He's greasy, he's clumsy, he's ape-like—"

"Only around you, Cara," Brian said. "I think you bring out the animal in him—"

"Worse than all those things—he's poor!"

Brian, for some odd reason, felt compelled to stick up for his cousin. "Come on, Cara. He's got some redeeming features. He gave my Jag a lube job. Now it purrs like a kitten. I was so pleased with the results, I tipped him an extra five bucks."

"He just wants your car to run well for when he steals it."

A lopsided grin drooped across Brian's face. "I hope not. I love that car." He cupped Cara's chin in his hand. "Almost as much as I love you," he added. Rebecca guessed he was lying. He cared more for his car than for anyone.

"But really, he's quite entertaining. Like taking a walk on

the wild side, know what I mean? Besides, he's not so bad once you get past his rough edges, although I'm not looking forward to being stuck with him all summer. I mean . . ." Brian moaned. "How am I going to explain him to my academy friends?"

"Is he staying at your house?" Rebecca asked.

"Oh, god!" Brian laughed. "Don't remind me. The maid put him into the room next to mine. I'll have to talk to her about moving him. Up all night with the TV blaring. He'll watch any sports show. Even Australian Rules Football. I think he's addicted to sports."

Brian looked at Cara, as if he had just remembered something. "Oh, by the way, tennis tomorrow at the country club?" Rebecca knew Brian was a superb tennis player. And for good reason—he had been taught by some of the best coaches money could buy.

"Love to," Cara said, affecting a British accent. For some reason, Rebecca had noticed, Cara always put on a phony English accent whenever the country club was mentioned. Cara was looking at her. "Perhaps you'd like to play some mixed doubles with us, Rebecca."

"Sure," Rebecca said, trying not to sound too eager. She loved to play tennis and the Cooper Hollow Country Club was the best club for miles around. She had been there a few times with Cara before and had been hoping for another invitation. It was a good place to meet guys.

"I guess you'll have to find your own doubles partner, then," Cara said in a slightly nasty tone of voice. Rebecca hadn't liked any of the guys Cara had fixed her up with as a doubles partner, and Cara took it personally.

"Let's meet at one. I have a facial in the morning," Brian said.

Brian was the only guy Rebecca knew who got a facial and wasn't embarrassed to admit it.

THE KILLING GAME

Rebecca excused herself to use the phone. It wouldn't be easy to find a doubles partner before tomorrow afternoon. She hurried to the row of public phones and yanked one off its cradle as she dug around in her bag for her address book and a quarter. In her haste, she dropped her bag and the contents spilled out onto the floor.

Rebecca cursed and let the phone drop as she knelt down and began to stuff her belongings back into her bag. She noticed a flyer on the ground—it must have fallen off the Night Owl bulletin board which hung on the wall next to the rest rooms. She stopped what she was doing to read it. It was an advertisement for a summer job. A man named Fletcher needed camp counselors at something called a "Survival Camp." Interesting. She pulled a pen from her purse and copied the phone number from the flyer as she sat there on the floor.

She stopped, pen poised in midair. Someone was standing right over her. Very close. Practically breathing on her. She glanced up her shoulder and saw Lee. "Oh!" she exclaimed. "You startled me."

"Sorry," he mumbled, wiping his wet hands and arms with a paper towel. He leaned down and picked up a lipstick. "Is this yours?"

"Oh, yeah, thanks," Rebecca smiled. She stood up and tacked the flyer back onto the bulletin board. There was an awkward silence as Lee kept his eyes on her face. Rebecca realized that he didn't know who she was. She tried to think of something to say to him—something to do with cars she could ask, but before she did, he broke the silence.

"May I borrow your pen for a moment?" Lee asked.

"Oh, sure," she said, handing it to him.

He tore off a piece of the paper towel, wrote something down on it, handed back her pen. Then he recognized her. "You're the girl at the booth—Cara's friend." She smiled. He eyed her warily. "I suppose I spilled something on you, too," he said, slightly defensive.

"Oh, no," Rebecca said with a little laugh. "I was just reading that flyer," she said, gesturing to the advertisement for survival camp counselors. "What do you suppose a survival camp is?"

Lee shrugged. "One way to find out."

"Are you looking for a summer job, too?" she asked.

"Yeah. As far away from Brian as I can get."

Rebecca chuckled.

A little pause.

"And you?" Lee asked.

"Yeah."

He fixed her with his dark gaze. "I'm sorry, I don't remember your name."

"Rebecca."

"Lee Spinelli." He reached out with a hand now free of grease and shook her own. He had a vise-like grip. "Are you doing anything this weekend?" he asked suddenly.

The question had caught her off guard. "I might be," she said hesitantly. "If I can find a tennis partner."

Lee looked at her sharply. "No kidding. My cousin's been bragging about what a great tennis player he is. I thought maybe if I could find a doubles partner I'd play him and his girlfriend this weekend. See for myself if he's as hot as he thinks he is. You wanna be my doubles partner?" There was a moment of silence. "Or are you afraid I might spill something on you?"

Rebecca smiled to herself. "Okay, it's a date."

"It's at his country club. The Cooper Hollow Country Club. I guess that's where all the snobs play their tennis. I'll meet you there at one. Okay?"

"Okay."

He nodded curtly and walked away.

She returned her attention to the flyer again. A Survival Camp. What exactly was a survival camp? She made sure she had written the number down correctly. Like Lee had said, there was one way to find out. There couldn't be any harm in giving this Fletcher guy a call.

Could there?

Two

Back at the dormitory that night Rebecca used the public phone at the end of the dorm hall to call the Survival Camp. Most girls went home for the weekend but Rebecca usually preferred to hang around the academy. It beat listening to her mother gripe about what a lousy world they lived in.

She called the number on the flyer and got a recording requesting an address to which to send a job application. She left her name and mail box number at the Cooper Riding Academy.

Then, she left Cara's name and home address as well.

The next afternoon, she had to listen to Cara's bitching during the drive to the country club. "I can't believe you would do this to me," she chastised Rebecca one more time.

Rebecca rolled her eyes and let out a sigh. Like she had agreed to have Lee as her tennis partner just to bug Cara. She cracked the passenger side window of Cara's tan BMW, letting the warm spring air wash over her. Maybe she could drown out Cara's words as well.

"Could you roll your window back up, please? I have the air conditioner on."

Rebecca did as she was told.

"Lee is nothing but trouble," Cara went on. "Why would you invite him to play doubles with us?"

"I told you, I didn't invite him, *he* invited *me*. If you had given me more time to find a doubles partner, maybe I could have found someone else."

"What was wrong with Biff Dexter?"

"He's a lousy tennis player."

Biff was a rich guy their age that Cara had introduced her to. He was also possibly the worst tennis player Rebecca had ever seen. Rebecca thought that Cara had fixed her up with Biff on purpose, to make sure Cara and Brian won the match. Both Cara and Brian were very good tennis players—and *very* poor losers.

Cara shook her head again. "After all I've done for you."

"What exactly have you done for me?"

"You've been meeting the right people," Cara reminded her. "It's not my fault you haven't followed through on any of them." Rebecca knew Cara was referring to Rebecca's reluctance to go all the way with any of the guys she went out with. Cara had such a strong sex drive, she couldn't imagine that any sixteen-year-old girl who had the opportunity to do otherwise would choose to remain a virgin.

Rebecca let her mind drift as Cara droned on. Cara had taken her to the country club several times and, true to her word, had introduced her to several young men from the upper crust of Cooper Hollow society. Every one a total dud. Most were virtual carbon copies of Brian. So into themselves they barely noticed you.

At least Brian played a mean game of tennis. Unfortunately, he never let you forget it. Nothing would give her more pleasure than ramming a tennis ball right into Brian's big mouth.

She wondered if Lee played tennis as well as he had played football. She doubted it. He just didn't have the build for it. His bruising physique was better suited for running over linebackers than serving up a tennis ball.

"I've got a great date lined up for you for the end-of-the-school-term ball if you're interested," Cara was saying. "Are you?"

"Huh?" Rebecca asked, her mind lingering on Lee.

"Earth to Rebecca. Are you interested in this date I have lined up for you for the end-of-the-school-term ball or not?"

"Not if it's another friend of Brian's from the academy," she answered honestly. Cadets were the worst dates as far as Rebecca was concerned. All that macho military stuff turned her off. And most of the cadets were as snooty as the girls from the Cooper Riding Academy they dated. For about the thousandth time since transferring from Cooper Hollow High to the riding academy, she wondered if she had made the right move. She just didn't feel comfortable around Cara and her friends, or the guys Cara set her up with.

"Okay, okay," Cara acknowledged. "I admit most of those guys have the personality of wallpaper, but this one's different," she said, beaming. "Besides, I think you already know him."

Cara enjoyed keeping Rebecca in suspense and paused meaningfully before continuing. "Guess who just dumped his little cheerleader girlfriend?" Cara asked.

Rebecca shrugged ambivalently. Despite what she had just told Cara, she wouldn't mind meeting the right rich guy and becoming Mrs. Moneybags, herself.

"Ross Peterson."

Rebecca felt her jaw drop. *The* Ross Peterson?"

Now this was different. Ross Peterson was the Hudson Military Academy's star quarterback on their unbeaten team, the handsome blond hunk who looked like a man among boys on the football field. His parents owned Peterson Bakeries which supplied breads and cakes to all the schools, stores, and restaurants in the area.

Cara nodded with a smirk. "The one and only High School

All-American Ross Peterson," Cara said, practically licking her lips as if Ross himself were a cinnamon sticky bun.

Cara gave the car a little gas and the BMW picked up speed. They were running a little late.

"Brian told me that Peterson's is *the* brand in New York City now. They just began distributing there last month. I'd get into some of his dough, myself, if I hadn't already invested so much time in his best friend, Brian McCracken." Cara gave Rebecca an appraising look. "Boy, the babies you and Ross could make with all those great genes floating around."

Rebecca looked away, slightly embarrassed.

"Shall I set it up, as if I had to ask?" Cara asked.

"I'm game," Rebecca said.

"You'll have to dump Lee."

"How can I dump a guy I'm not even dating?"

"You know what I mean. After today, he's history. I can't be setting you up with primo guys like Ross Peterson if you're seen with low-lifes like Lee Smellnelli."

Rebecca shook her head in dismay. "Why do you hate Lee so much? Just because he ruined your brand new Donna Karan cashmere sweater."

"I don't *hate* him," Cara protested. "And it has nothing to do with my sweater. He's just not right for you. Trust me. Brian tolerates him only because his father will cut his allowance if he doesn't. Lee's trouble."

"Come on, Cara," Rebecca said, losing patience. "That sounds so melodramatic. He's probably just a regular guy who doesn't go to a fancy prep school or have a lot of money. Like a zillion other teenagers."

"*Normal* teenage boys don't get arrested for stealing cars," Cara countered.

"You mean Lee really went to jail?" Rebecca tried to picture Lee behind bars.

"Well," Cara said, "I don't think he actually *served time*. But he definitely has some criminal type friends. And I heard some rumors about him and a girl . . ."

Now, Rebecca really was interested. "What happened?" she asked, her eyes wide.

Cara paused dramatically. "I heard he beat up his ex-girlfriend. Then he smashed her cars to bits."

Rebecca was appalled. But even though Lee did seem tough, he hadn't struck Rebecca as being so brutal. She decided to take what Cara told her with a grain of salt. She would be wary of Lee, but try not to prejudge him. After all, Cara's relationship with the truth wasn't always so close. She decided to give Lee the benefit of the doubt.

They pulled into the parking lot of the Cooper Hollow Country Club. Cara parked her car next to Brian's silver Jaguar and they hurried to the locker room to change. A few minutes later, they found Brian and Lee already on the court hitting the ball around.

Rebecca watched Brian deliver a backhand with a smooth-as-silk motion. He looked like a junior circuit player, dressed in white from head to toe, his high tech racket flashing through the air to meet the ball with a resounding thwack.

Then she checked out Lee. He was wearing a pair of ratty red gym shorts with white trim, a black, heavy metal T-shirt, and black, hightop sneakers with no socks. His muscular biceps bulged from beneath his shirt. He looked more like a blacksmith than a tennis player. His racket looked like something he had found at the bottom of a box at the Salvation Army.

The boys took a break when they saw the girls and came over to greet them. Rebecca watched Lee as he crossed the court, his walk more an arrogant swagger than a stride, as if daring someone to cross his path.

"Ladies," Brian said in salutation, grabbing a towel to wipe

THE KILLING GAME

the sweat from his face and arms. The sun was high in a solid blue sky, and the heat beat down on them. "Lee and I were just knocking the old pellet around." He looked at Lee. "You've got a lot of power, cuz, I'll grant you that much, but you're lacking in technique."

"I'm still a bit rusty," Lee conceded. "I haven't played since I picked up a football. Basically, tennis is for wimps."

Brian chuckled. "We'll see who's the wimp after today's game."

"Yeah, I guess we will, won't we," Lee said, his eyes boring into Brian.

"Perhaps after Cara and I crush you, I'll give you a few lessons. Since I'm stuck with you for the summer anyway," Brian said with a patronizing smile. "But you'll have to use another racket. Perhaps I'll loan you one of my extras."

"After today's game," Lee said to Brian, "you'll be asking *me* for lessons."

Brian laughed loudly. "Really, cuz. Do you think you could beat me?"

"Yeah."

"At doubles?"

"At anything."

"A hundred dollars says you're mistaken."

"You're on," Lee said without a moment's hesitation.

They walked to their separate ends of the court to warm up. Lee sidled up to Rebecca and said, "Are you any good, by the way?"

"I can hold my own," Rebecca said modestly.

"That's good," Lee said. "Because I don't have any money."

Rebecca felt uneasy. Did that bet include her? She didn't have any money, either.

They warmed up. Lee let her take most of the shots since he had already broken a sweat. The shots he did take were pretty erratic, usually ending up in the net or bouncing off the back fence.

Lee saw her studying him. "Don't worry. I'm never very good warming up."

Brian served first, as confident as ever, and he and Cara easily won the first game on Lee's unforced error.

Lee retrieved the ball as Brian strode to the opposite deuce court to receive the serve. Lee walked up to Rebecca and shrugged sheepishly. "I'm still getting warmed up." Rebecca smiled weakly. Lee tossed her the ball. "Hit it right at him, if you can. I noticed his stroke's a bit weak if he can't extend his arm."

Rebecca nodded. She hit the ball flat and right at Brian. He stepped back and returned the ball with a crimped back hand. Lee calmly intercepted the ball and bashed it into the open court past Cara for a winner.

Brian began to look a little worried as Rebecca and Lee won the second game without losing a point. Both sides stayed on serve until set point.

At 40–30 Brian prepared to serve for the set, with Lee receiving. He paused and looked at Lee with supreme confidence. "You've played well, cuz. Better than I thought. But the time has come for you to meet your master."

Rebecca cringed. Brian was such a blowhard. And Lee *had* played well. It was true his game lacked style, but he had won several games outright with powerful forehands. She was determined not to let Brian and Cara win this point. She prayed Brian wouldn't serve an ace.

Brian tossed the ball high into the air. With a vengeance, he whipped the racket around and hit the ball flat, with plenty of weight behind it, and sent a rocket toward Lee. Lee managed to block the shot. The ball drifted lazily over the net where Cara met it and mashed it.

Like lightning, Rebecca was on the ball and volleyed it

back to Cara. Cara smacked the ball back at her, and for a brief exchange, the game resembled a ping pong match. Then Cara hit a beautiful topspin lob to the far corner.

Lee tracked the ball down just in time and got it back over the net. The ball fell nicely on the opposite baseline. Brian easily reached it and, with triumph dripping all over his smirking face, hit a two-handed back hand that had winner written all over it.

Rebecca charged the net to intercept and just got her racket on it. A surprised Brian sliced it back. Rebecca took it in midair and banged the ball past a lunging Cara for the point.

The game went to deuce.

Brian was all business now. He served to Rebecca. The ball hooked into the service court with plenty of topspin, surprising Rebecca, who expected a power shot on the first serve. She blocked it weakly and sent a lollipop back to Brian. He blasted a forehand back over the net.

The ball bounced fair with plenty of topspin and looked out of reach, but now it was Lee who appeared out of nowhere to intercept the ball. He screeched a forehand of his own that had Brian racing toward the baseline to intercept it. Brian returned the ball and Lee screamed another forehand back to him.

Now Cara was forced to retreat from the net to cover the baseline in the face of Lee's forehand onslaught. Brian returned a weak defensive lob. Lee took it on one high hop, disguised an overhand smash, and drop-shot the ball with wicked backspin, barely clearing the top of the net. The ball fell fair into the portion of the court just vacated by the retreating Cara.

It was a beautiful, almost impossible shot.

Lee chortled loudly. "How's that for technique, *cuz?*" he shouted to a tight-lipped Brian.

Brian turned red.

Cara was glowering.

Rebecca was looking at Lee with newfound admiration.

Advantage to Rebecca and Lee. They took the first set when Lee hit a vicious overhand smash off Cara's nose. Her Ray Bans clattered to the court surface from the impact. "You did that on purpose!" Cara shouted at Lee, holding her nose, checking for blood.

Lee offered no apologies.

Cara slammed her racket into the net and stormed off the court.

Lee swaggered up to Brian. "I guess your partner's conceding. You owe us a hundred dollars, *cuz*."

Brian muttered something obscene, packed his gear in silence, and trudged off in the direction of the locker room without looking back.

Rebecca shook hands with Lee. "You were great," she said. "Where'd you learn to play like that?"

Lee only shrugged, picking at a broken string on his dilapidated racket. "Sports have always come easy to me, I guess. I'm just lucky that way."

Rebecca looked off in the direction of the clubhouse. "Well . . . I guess I better go catch up to Cara or I'll be walking home." She gathered up Cara's Ray Bans and racket and hurried to the clubhouse. "Bye."

"Bye."

She hurried to the women's locker room, fighting off a feeling of regret. She wanted to stay and chat with Lee, but if she did, she had the feeling it would be the end of her friendship with Cara. And the end of her opportunity to go out with Ross Peterson.

Lee was definitely cute, but like Cara had said before, he was not right for her. He had a nowhere life, and going out with him would take her in the same direction.

She ran into the steamy locker room. She didn't see Cara

anywhere. She quickly showered and headed for the snack bar. She didn't see her there, either. She hurried into the parking lot. As she suspected, Cara's car was missing.

So was Brian's silver Jag.

A shadow fell across her. She turned around and saw Lee standing behind her, his dark curly hair still damp from the shower.

"Did you lose your ride, too?" he asked her.

"Yeah." She shrugged, then smiled. "Sore losers, I guess." They stared at each other for a long, awkward moment. "Well . . ." Rebecca said at last. "Shall I call a cab?" It was a long walk back to the riding academy.

"It'll have to be your treat. Brian didn't stick around long enough to pay off on the bet."

Rebecca hesitated. She didn't have the money for a cab, either. "I, ah . . . left my bag back at the dormitory."

"Your bag's around your shoulder."

"I meant my bag with the money in it. Actually, I'm broke."

"Oh." Lee dug around in his pocket and came out with a handful of loose change and counted it. "Well . . . I got just enough for two bus fares. My treat."

She smiled, thanked Lee, and followed him to the bus stop that stood right outside the country club. Rebecca's bag slipped off her shoulder and Lee placed it back for her, gently. His arm rested on her shoulder for a moment, then slipped down to her arm.

Rebecca didn't want to be rude and shrug off his arm, but she hoped no one she knew would see them. If this got back to Cara, she could kiss Ross Peterson goodbye before she even met him.

She looked down the street, hoping to see a bus, but saw none. She sighed and was about to step back onto the curb when Lee roughly pulled her backwards. An old, battered Chevy roared past them.

"That jerk almost hit me," she screamed. She would have been dead if Lee hadn't pulled her back onto the curb.

Suddenly the driver slammed on the brakes, startling Rebecca. The car burned rubber as it backed up.

Oh, no, Rebecca thought, he wants a second chance to kill me.

Three

The car screeched to a stop in a cloud of smelly, rubbery smoke. "Hey, baby," said the evil-looking sleazeball in the passenger seat. He leered at her, displaying a missing front tooth. Rebecca could smell the alcohol on his breath from a yard away. She hoped she wouldn't ever get any closer than that.

Rebecca's heart was thumping away in her chest. "I think we'd better run," she muttered.

Lee laughed. "It's cool. They're friends of mine."

Uh-oh, thought Rebecca. Maybe Cara's stories were true. The guys in the car *did* look like criminals.

Lee went up to the guy in the front passenger seat and shook hands through the window. Rebecca noticed the guy had a tattoo of a snake on his wrist. His dark kinky hair shot out from beneath a broad brimmed hat that had a feather stuck in its band.

"What's happening, Lee?" the guy with the tattoo asked.

"Not much. What's happening with you?"

"Just cruising. You wanna come along for a ride?"

He glanced over his shoulder at Rebecca. "Nah, better not."

The guy with the tattoo looked around Lee, at Rebecca. "Who's she?"

"A friend."

The sleazes hooted and smirked. "So, what are you and your *friend* doing here?"

"Waiting for the bus."

"What happened to your wheels?"

"I got a lift over here, but my ride left without me."

The guy with the tattoo looked at the country club, standing majestically behind the tall wrought iron fence that surrounded it. "You were in there? At the Cooper Hollow Country Club?" He pushed his nose in the air with one finger as he said the name of the club.

"Yeah," Lee said a little sheepishly.

Tattoo and the other guy laughed derisively.

"Doing what?" Tattoo asked.

Lee held up his pummeled tennis racket. "Playing tennis. What else."

The guys thought that was pretty funny and were laughing and hooting and slapping each other on the back some more.

"The country club," Tattoo snorted. "I got some relatives that go there."

"Really?" asked Lee.

"Yeah. They go there to wash the dishes and take out the garbage." This brought on more laughter. This time Lee joined in. Rebecca looked down the street praying for a bus to arrive soon. She'd just borrow the fare from Lee and get away from these Neanderthals.

"You want a ride somewhere?" asked the driver. Lee hadn't bothered to introduce his friends to Rebecca, for which Rebecca was grateful. She didn't want these delinquents to know her name.

Lee hesitated.

"Come on. This bus you're waiting for comes along about once a year, you know," Tattoo added.

Still Lee hesitated. Rebecca figured it was out of consideration for her.

THE KILLING GAME

"What's the matter Mr. Country Club?" his friend goaded him. "Suddenly we're not good enough for you? Maybe I should go get my clubs and come back so we can get in a few holes of golf while we wait for the bus."

Lee grinned. He patted his pal on the arm, stood up, looked back at Rebecca. "Come on, we've got a ride."

Rebecca hesitated, a bit unnerved. "I think I'll just wait here if you don't mind lending me some money for the bus."

"It'll be fine," Lee said with a reassuring smile, taking her gently by the arm. "It's hot out here and there's no telling when the next bus is coming."

Rebecca hesitated and Lee seemed to sense her fear. "C'mon, I know these guys," he said. "They're all right. They're friends of mine."

Rebecca smiled weakly. "Okay," she said without conviction.

Lee nodded to the guy with the tattoo and opened the car door. Tattoo got out and looked Rebecca up and down before climbing into the back seat. Rebecca slid in the front seat, tightly gripping her own and Cara's tennis rackets. Lee followed.

Rebecca glanced into the backseat and saw three frightening individuals staring back at her. She also saw the bus coming over the hill.

She was about to mention the bus to Lee when the driver, a huge guy with a mop of dirty brown hair, mashed down on the gas pedal. She was pinned to the seat as tires squealed, laying down twin patches of rubber. The passenger door slammed shut from the force of the acceleration.

So much for catching the bus.

Rebecca felt around for a seat belt but found none. She glanced over at Lee who was smiling contentedly, totally at ease, as the Cooper Hollow Country Club zipped past their window. She glanced over at the driver, who was looking at her with a lopsided grin.

The driver took a plug from a quart size bottle of beer he had jammed between his legs. He offered Rebecca a hit, which she politely refused.

"Rebecca," Lee said, pointing to the driver, "the big guy driving is Shorty, and the three guys in the back are Larry, Curly, and Moe."

Laughter from the back. The guy in the front flashed her a shy, friendly smile which compensated for his menacing appearance. When the laughter subsided, Lee said, "Actually, that's Mike driving and the three guys in the back are Snake, Looney, and Bobby."

Rebecca looked over her shoulder and gave the guys in the back a friendly nod. The one in the middle called Looney had huge ears which stuck straight out from his head and made him look truly looney. Bobby appeared to be in a catatonic state, or perhaps he was just drunk or high on something.

Snake, the guy with the snake tattoo, leered at her. Rebecca turned to face the front again.

"I hear you got expelled from school," Snake said to Lee from the backseat.

"Yeah," Lee said, anger entering his voice. "I've got to do my senior year all over again thanks to *her.*"

Rebecca wondered if they were talking about Lee's ex-girlfriend. The one Cara said he beat up.

"You can't graduate through summer school?" Mike asked. He looked to be a few years older than the rest.

"Nah. I've got to get a summer job. Part of my plea bargain."

"That sucks," Mike said.

Snake laughed. "You ought to mess that little bitch up." Rebecca moved uneasily on her seat. "Seriously, man. We'll help if you want us to."

"Forget it," Lee said. "That's not my thing."

Rebecca heard the flick of a lighter and smelled a heavy, sweet aroma. She glanced nervously over her shoulder. Snake had lit a joint and was passing it to Looney.

Rebecca felt a tap on her shoulder which made her jump. She turned around and saw Snake with the joint stuck between the gap in his teeth. He reminded her of Harpo Marx for some reason, and Rebecca almost laughed. Snake took her smile as encouragement and pointed to the lit joint as if offering her a toke. Lee glanced over his shoulder. "Knock it off, Snake. She doesn't do stuff like that. She goes to the riding academy."

Rebecca was offended by Lee's remark. Just because she attended the riding academy didn't mean she was a total square. "I'll try some," she said.

Lee shrugged as if to say it was nothing to him one way or the other, but Rebecca sensed that he disapproved. Snake passed her the joint. "You don't have to prove anything to those guys. Just give it to Mike if you don't want any."

"I smoke pot all the time," Rebecca lied. Actually, she had smoked pot exactly twice with almost no effect whatsoever. Mostly it just burned her throat and left an unpleasant taste in her mouth. She took a big hit from the joint and immediately coughed it all out.

Lee clucked disapprovingly. The others laughed, except Bobby, who remained in his coma. She took another, smaller hit and passed the joint to Lee. He waved it away.

"You going straight now, bro?" Snake asked Lee.

"Got to. They're testing me for drugs when I rejoin the team next fall. Part of my plea bargain."

"That's next fall."

"Yeah, I know, but the stuff stays in the blood for awhile."

"Wimp." Looney said from the back seat.

Lee ripped the joint from Rebecca's hand, who still held

it dumbly, and handed it to Mike. Mike took a massive hit before passing it back to Snake.

Rebecca suddenly felt dizzy. She started to feel paranoid. It was getting hard to see in the car, with all the smoke. She slipped on Cara's Ray Bans.

Snake chuckled from the back seat. "Did you get a buzz, baby?"

Is he talking to me? Rebecca wondered.

Snake chuckled again.

They were racing down Thirteen Bends Road with Mike shifting expertly through the gears between hits of the joint and swigs of his beer.

She refused the joint when it was offered to her again and wished she hadn't smoked what she had. She looked up in time to see a tree come flying out of nowhere and braced for the impact.

Mike whipped the steering wheel around and the car snaked through a curve, the wheels howling for relief. Rebecca gripped the edge of the seat as Mike swerved around one perilous curve after another. So this was her punishment for getting into the car. She was going to die a horrible death in a fiery crash. She had heard that burning to death was probably the most painful way to go.

"Where we going, anyway?" Mike asked Lee.

Lee looked at Rebecca. "Where we going?" he repeated.

Rebecca lived south of Old Wilson Highway, in the poor section of Cooper Hollow, but she didn't want Lee or anyone else to know that. "Ah, you can just let me off at the Riding Academy."

"Right," Mike said.

They were near the Night Owl Club. "Hey, Mikey," Lee said. "Stop by the club just for a second, would ya? I want to see if my cousin's inside. The dude owes me a hundred bucks. Lunch is on me if he's there."

A small cheer from the back seat.

Mike needed no further convincing. Snake and Looney hurriedly finished off the joint, filling the car with even more smoke. Mike turned into the Night Owl parking lot and looked for a spot. He cut into what he thought was an empty slot and banged into the front of a car.

Heads jolted forward as Mike braked sharply. Metal on metal groaned as the fenders made contact. The tinted driver's side window of the struck car smoothly slid down. A head poked out the window.

Rebecca's heart skipped a beat.

It was Brian. Mike had hit Brian's Jag.

Four

"Where'd you get your license, asshole!" Brian shouted to Mike.

Mike put the car into park and removed his large bulky frame from behind the steering wheel. Through the haze of pot smoke still clinging to the air, Rebecca watched Mike march toward the driver's side of Brian's car.

Rebecca watched as Brian's smartass expression turned to one of fear as Mike reached through the open driver side window and pulled him through it. With one strong hand he held Brian dangling in the air.

Lee bolted from the car, followed by the others, leaving Rebecca alone in the car.

"Yo, Mike, cool it man! That's my cousin!" Lee said.

"He should learn some manners," Mike growled, still dangling Brian in the air.

The passenger side door of Brian's Jag flew open and Cara bounced out, buttoning up her blouse and straightening her tennis skirt. It was then that Rebecca noticed Cara's BMW was parked right next to Brian's Jag. She felt the blood drain from her face.

Rebecca ducked down beneath the dashboard, her heart pounding inside her chest as if it were about to burst. She expected any moment to hear Cara's footsteps stampeding across the Night Owl parking lot to find her hiding there on the floor of a battered Chevy filled with marijuana smoke.

If that happened, she was finished! She would never get to go out with Ross Peterson.

She heard Cara arguing with Mike. Rebecca breathed a deep sigh of relief. She hadn't seen her after all.

Cara's loud and abrasive voice filled the parking lot. She was threatening to call the cops from her car phone if Mike didn't put Brian down right this very second.

Rebecca peeked over the dashboard and saw Mike unceremoniously drop Brian to the ground. An angry Brian scrambled to his feet and glared at Lee. "What's the meaning of this?" he demanded, dusting the parking lot grime off his Nike tennis whites.

"You owe me a hundred bucks, cuz," Lee said.

"That's why you roughed me up?"

"The rough stuff's between you and Mike. Just pay *me* the hundred bucks you owe me."

Grumbling, but clearly intimidated, Brian reached into his pocket and pulled out his wallet. He peeled off two fifty dollar bills and tossed them onto the ground. Lee looked hard at Brian, as he knelt and picked up the money. Then he turned and walked back toward the car.

Rebecca's heart jumped into her throat as she ducked down beneath the dashboard again.

"Rebecca!" Lee's voice bellowed from above her. She looked up and saw his dark eyes staring down at her. He thrust a fifty dollar bill through the open passenger side window. "Your half of the bet money."

Rebecca smiled sheepishly. "Ah . . . thanks Lee, that's okay, you keep it," she whispered.

"Are you all right?" Lee asked. "Why are you whispering? And what are you doing down there. Did you lose something?"

Then she saw Cara's face appear at the window. "Rebecca? What *are* you doing down there?"

* * *

A few days later, Rebecca was lying on her bed in her dorm room feeling sorry for herself. Classes were done for the day, and Rebecca had nothing to do.

After the fiasco in the parking lot at the Night Owl word had gotten around the school—passed on by Cara, no doubt—that Rebecca had joined Lee Spinelli's gang of punks. The same gang that had mugged Brian McCracken and stolen a hundred dollars from him.

Cara, and most of the other girls, had been avoiding her ever since. It didn't matter that it wasn't true. Cara Worthington said it, and the girls at the riding academy believed it.

So Cara and the other girls had been giving her the cold shoulder, which was hard for Cara to do since they shared the same dorm room. But Cara always had a way of getting around the rules. She had apparently found sleeping arrangements elsewhere and when they had classes together, Cara continued to give her the old-fashioned silent treatment.

And to make matters worse, girls like Cara had a long memory. Rebecca knew life was going to be hell for her at the riding academy if she didn't patch things up with her. Maybe when Cara returned from Europe or China or wherever she was going, things would get back to normal. By then Lee would be history.

Or would he?

She had to admit she was spending a lot of time daydreaming about Lee. With his dark glowing eyes and his mane of black curly hair brushing her face, he was on her mind even when she slept, and kept appearing in her dreams. She was having a hard time sorting out her feelings over Lee. She liked him, but he and his friends scared her. Besides, she was still hoping to meet some rich country club boy she could stand to be with for more than two minutes, who would whisk her away to Paris for the summer.

Rebecca loved equestrian, as she did most sports, but obviously riding horses was not going to get her ahead in the world. The Cooper Riding Academy was, for her, a stepping stone. A place to meet rich girls who knew rich guys.

She hated being poor. Her biggest fear in life was to end up like her mother. A poor woman scratching out a meager living in a nowhere job, before returning home to her gin bottle and her nowhere life. Alone, except on the weekends, when Rebecca returned home from the academy.

And lately, Rebecca had been spending her weekends at the academy. She felt a little guilty about leaving her mother alone, but it sure beat the pain she felt watching her mother drink herself to death.

No, she couldn't bear that. It was better to just try to live her own life at the Riding Academy until . . . until what? Till her prince, a knight in shining armor, would come and rescue her?

Rebecca was beginning to get depressed thinking about her dismal opportunities for the future. And she was bored lazing around her dormitory room by herself.

Rebecca realized that she hadn't checked her mailbox recently. She wasn't in the habit of checking her mail everyday because she rarely got any mail. But then she remembered calling the number for the survival camp and requesting a job application. Maybe it had arrived.

She slipped on her sneakers and made her way down the dorm wing to the main building of the academy where the mailboxes were. She checked the row of mail slots. Sheridan, Silverman, Stewart, Swenson—it was there! She pulled it out and ripped open the envelope, reading as she walked back to her room.

It was the oddest job application she had ever seen, and

she had seen a lot of them in the past few years. The generic cover letter stressed the need to be in top physical condition. This camp must be pretty rugged, she thought. The application didn't ask for grades or references, but it did have several lines reserved for a list of any awards won in athletic competition.

Rebecca listed her scholarship at the Cooper Riding Academy as well as the various trophies and ribbons she had won on the swimming team at Cooper Hollow High.

The were some other questions and she answered them all. The oddest question of all was the size of her head. Now, why would they want to know something like that? She didn't *know* the size. She shrugged and wrote down *medium*.

When she was done, she put the application in the pre-addressed return envelope and sent it off to a post office box in Maine. Rebecca had put off looking into other job possibilities. She hoped the camp would hire her—otherwise she might end up loading trucks for Brian's father's business. Ugh!

There was only one week left until summer break and the annual Ball, but Rebecca didn't think she'd be going to the Ball with Ross Peterson.

Or anyone else.

A few days later, Rebecca walked down to the main building of the academy to check the mail. There was a letter waiting for her. From Maine! She eagerly tore it open and a large postcard fell out. She had been selected as a counselor for the EDWARD FLETCHER SURVIVAL CAMP. One of only six from hundreds of applicants.

Far out!

She flipped the card over.

Pig Island.

THE KILLING GAME

Weird name for an island. She took a closer look at the postcard. Pig Island was a remote island off the New England coast. *Very* remote, it appeared, from the postcard. And kind of desolate looking. More fitting for goats than campers, actually, it seemed to her. Or pigs. Well . . . it was only a postcard.

She flipped the card over again. The back was crammed with information in small print. She read on.

She had to bring her own camping gear!

She hadn't figured on that. She didn't have any camping gear. And she didn't have any money to buy it, either. Oh, well, she'd solve that problem later, assuming she didn't change her mind completely about this survival camp business. The living conditions on the island were probably very primitive—outhouses, cold water showers.

But the money was good. In fact, it was great. By far the most money she had ever made at a summer job. And it was only for two months.

What did she have to lose?

She decided to hike over to the Night Owl Club. She was curious to see if any other kids from Cooper Hollow had been chosen as camp counselors.

She took the path through the dense woods that led from the riding academy to the Night Owl Club, debating on the way the pros and cons of a summer spent on a remote island. But other thoughts kept creeping uninvited into her mind. Horrible thoughts of bloody violence, unbelievable accidents, and murders—things that were rumored to have happened in these woods near the Night Owl Club. These woods always spooked Rebecca whenever she walked through them. But it was the quickest way to get to the Night Owl Club. Besides, she reasoned, she had to get used to walking in the woods—she'd be doing a lot of hiking this summer at camp.

Still, she was relieved when she emerged into the parking

lot of the Night Owl Club. Once inside, she posted a note on the bulletin board addressed to all survival camp counselors. It suggested they meet for a "get together party" the following Friday night, at the Night Owl. The meeting place would be a corner table in the dance room.

Camp counselors were to be picked up from a pier in Maine the following Monday night and taken by ferry to Pig Island. She would need a ride to the pick-up spot as well as some camping gear.

She realized that there was no longer any doubt in her mind that she would take the job.

Well, why not? She needed a break from the boredom and the strict discipline of the riding academy—and from Cara's abuse. Besides, the money was too good to turn down.

Survival Camp.

She had never heard of such a thing, but there was no harm in giving it a try. If she absolutely hated it, she would just come home early.

Five

It was Friday night at the Night Owl and the band was just finishing up a set. It was a heavy metal band and the crowd was really into the music. Unfortunately, the table Rebecca had chosen for a meeting place was right next to the speakers. The lead guitar player hit a high note on his jet black Gibson Les Paul electric guitar and the note screamed right into the center of Rebecca's brain.

She was already on edge, and the music wasn't helping any. She had just had a big argument with her mother about going away for the summer. Rebecca knew her mother was dependent on her and that she would be lonely without Rebecca to talk to. But Rebecca resented her mother's selfishness. Other parents let their children grow up and have their own lives—why couldn't her mother do the same? Rebecca knew the answer: because her mother was an alcoholic. Still, Rebecca knew it wasn't her fault her mother was sick, and she was determined not to let her mother ruin her life. Survival camp couldn't be tougher than her home life, Rebecca consoled herself.

To pass the time, she looked out on the dance floor at the couples gyrating to the loud music. Some were rubbing up against each other so furiously she imagined their clothes going up in a burst of passionate flames. Others maintained a safe distance from each other. As she scanned the dancers, one figure held her gaze. Rebecca caught her breath. *Ross*

Peterson. Ross was dancing with a girl Rebecca knew from school. She was a year behind Rebecca, one of the many Cara wannabees who sucked up to Cara in the hopes of getting a date with someone like Ross. Rebecca fought back the jealousy she felt creeping up her body. That could have been me dancing with Ross, she thought.

The band went on a break.

It was getting late and no other camp counselors had shown up yet. If there even *were* any from Cooper Hollow. She shifted anxiously in her chair. Rebecca was naturally shy, and it had always been difficult for her to meet new people. She hoped she would feel a little more comfortable if she had at least a passing acquaintance with some of the other counselors with whom she was going to spend the entire summer on a remote island in the most primitive of conditions.

A large shadow fell over the table. Rebecca looked up at the form looming in front of her. He was big, even bigger than Lee's friend Mike. He seemed to be about her age, with fat legs and a rear end to match. His head was as round as a canteloupe, and his hair was shaved close to the skull; it stood up on end, like the bristles on a worn scrub brush.

He had Hudson Military Academy written all over his face.

"Is this the survival camp table?" he asked, knocking over a chair. He picked up the chair and held on to it to steady himself.

"Yeah." No use chickening out now, Rebecca thought, as she tried to psyche herself up to talk to the guy. After all, she had posted the note; now she had to act as a kind of host.

He sat in the chair opposite her without saying another word and stared at the table top. His broad face was a sick, pasty color. She was about to try to start a conversation when she saw Brian McCracken staggering toward her table with a basket full of greasy fries, smothered in ketchup. Both Brian and the large fellow staring at the table top were obviously in the latter stages of a serious, end-of-the-school-term party night.

The big guy looked up briefly. "This is the table, Bri."

Brian stopped short when he saw Rebecca. "What are *you* doing here?"

"Nice to see you, too, Brian," Rebecca answered sarcastically. Brian had been keeping his distance from Rebecca lately. Not that Rebecca had missed his company.

"You're not part of the survival camp business, are you?"

" 'Fraid so."

It took only a moment for Brian to regain his composure, and return to his usual smug self. "This large piece of meat is Kevin Kilroy," Brian said, by way of introduction, fondly and drunkenly wrapping his arm around the big boy's massive shoulders. "A fellow cadet—"

"And bodyguard," Kevin interjected.

"And bodyguard. We cadets stick together, right Kev?"

"Right, Bri. If the price is right—"

"There will be no more incidents like the one in the Night Owl parking lot when you and your friends ganged up on me."

"We didn't gang up on you. And they're not *my* friends. They're *your cousin's* friends." Rebecca was sick and tired of taking all the blame for what had happened in the parking lot the previous week.

Brian turned to Kevin. "And this is Rebecca Swenson. She's in that gang of thugs that roughed me up—"

"I am not in anyone's gang," Rebecca protested. "I hardly know Lee, much less those guys he was with."

Brian winced when he heard Lee's name mentioned. He removed a flask from his back pocket, looked around, and took a slug when the coast was clear. Then he wiped the back of his mouth with a slender, delicate hand. He nudged

Kevin with his elbow and offered him the flask under the table.

Kevin shook his head no.

Brian chuckled wickedly. "I told you I could drink you under the table—anytime, anyplace—big guy. No one—but no one—can outdrink a McCracken." He took another slug from the flask before capping it and placing it back in his pocket.

Rebecca was having second thoughts about the survival camp.

Brian looked at Rebecca with bloodshot, bleary eyes. "Oh, I'm sorry," he said, pulling out the flask and offering it to Rebecca. "Care for a shot?"

"No, thanks," Rebecca said with a weak smile.

He pushed the basket of fries at Kevin, who continued to stare mutely at the table. "Eat up, Kev, we'll need our strength this summer if we're to *survive.*"

Then he looked at Rebecca and said in a serious, macho voice, "You don't know what survival is until you've gone through your freshman year at the Hudson Military Academy. If you can survive that, you can survive anything." He looked over at Kevin. "Right, Kev?"

Kevin abruptly stood up, his chair banging to the floor. "I think I have to puke."

Brian gave Kev a little salute. "Don't get lost in there." Kevin hurried away. Brian looked at Rebecca and shrugged. "You'd puke too if you ate academy food." He looked about the crowded club. "Seen Cara anywhere?"

"She's *your* girlfriend."

"I wonder sometimes."

"Trouble in paradise?"

"It's hard to tell with her, if you know what I mean."

Rebecca did.

"You rich bitches at the riding academy are hard to figure out."

"I'm no rich bitch," Rebecca said defensively. "I'm there on scholarship, remember?"

But Brian continued as if she hadn't said anything. "Not that I have anything against rich bitches." He held up both hands. "Why, after all, my very own mother is a rich bitch and I wouldn't be here without her."

Then he leaned forward until his face was inches from hers. "Let me ask you something." Rebecca was repulsed by his awful breath. "Are all the girls at the academy as horny as Cara Worthington?"

Rebecca's already low opinion of Brian was sinking more with each minute. She leaned back to get some fresh air. "Absolutely, Bri. It's because we go to an all girls school. Why, every full moon we dance naked down by the lake and have a full scale orgy and lesbian sex."

Brian slammed his hand upon the table top, nearly toppling the small bowl that held the lit candle. "I knew it!"

The lit candle suddenly went out.

Rebecca looked over her shoulder and saw a girl about her own age standing there. She had shaggy, dark brown hair that fell across much of her face. The girl pushed her hair to the side, revealing a pair of extraordinarily large, doe-like eyes. "Is this the table for the Fletcher Survival Camp?"

Rebecca nodded and the girl took a seat at the table. She was slender and pale and wearing what could only be described as a chic-gypsy-sixties-hippie outfit, with army boots a Hudson Military Academy cadet would be proud of. "My name's Melanie Anderson."

"Glad to meet you, Melanie," Rebecca said. "This is Brian. My name's Rebecca. Kevin, another guy going to the camp with us, is in the bathroom, puking."

Melanie looked at Brian, whose face had suddenly taken

on the same pasty color as Kevin's. He suddenly stood up and staggered in the direction of the john. Melanie watched him go before looking back at Rebecca. "Are all the camp counselors here?"

As if on cue, Cara Worthington suddenly strode through the arched doorway and made a beeline to their table.

Rebecca smiled bravely.

Cara stared at her for a long time with a look of malice so cold it coated the air with frost. "I better not have the right table."

"Are you a survival camp counselor?" Melanie asked pleasantly.

The air grew even chillier. "I wondered who sent that job application to my house." Her eyes bore into Rebecca as she pointed a long, sharp red fingernail at her. "Now I know!" She turned on her heels and stormed angrily away.

Melanie looked quizzically at Rebecca. "Is she a friend of yours?"

"She used to be," Rebecca said by way of explanation.

Melanie shrugged, then excused herself to use the bathroom.

Rebecca watched her walk away and wondered if she would ever see her again. Perhaps Melanie was thinking the same thing she was—that this survival camp business wasn't such a hot idea, after all. So far, the counselors-to-be hadn't exactly hit it off during their little "get together."

The band was back on stage, getting ready to play another set. Rebecca looked up and saw Lee walking toward her.

"I had a funny feeling you were the one who left that note," he said. "I remembered you reading the flyer on the bulletin board the first day we met. Was I right? Are we camp counselors in crime together this summer?"

"Yeah," Rebecca said with a grin.

"Cool. Are you excited about going?"

"I guess so." If she was still going. "But I don't have any camping gear. Do you think they'll turn me away if I show up empty-handed?"

Lee waved away her fears. "Brian has plenty, don't worry about it. Oh . . . did you know Brian's coming along, too?"

Rebecca moaned. "Now, I know. And one of his cadet friends. And *Cara*."

"Cara!"

"That's right."

"No way Cara's going to spend the summer at some primitive wilderness camp. The only islands she would go to are in the Caribbean, and she'd be staying at a luxury hotel. The only reason Brian's coming along is because his father's making him do it to keep an eye on me. To make sure I keep out of trouble."

"On an island? What kind of trouble can you get into on a remote island in the middle of nowhere?"

"Tell me about it. I've been arguing with my uncle all week about that but he's making Brian go anyway. I think he just wants to get rid of him for the summer and is using me as an excuse. But anyway, Uncle Pete bought us both a ton of camping gear. All new, I might add. I have a station wagon, too, so we'll have plenty of room for our gear. I've been working on it all week. I rescued it from a junkyard—but it should get us there. I mean . . . if you want to catch a ride with me."

"Sure." She thought of Melanie. She might also need a ride. "Does this station wagon have enough room for another passenger?"

Lee shook his head. "I'm not taking Brian with us. It's bad enough that I'll have to spend the entire summer with him—"

"Not Brian. There's another girl besides Cara that's—" Just then, Melanie returned to the table. "Lee, do you know Melanie? She's going to be a camp counselor with us this summer."

Lee's expression turned hard and his smile disappeared. If looks could kill, they'd already be ordering Melanie's casket. Lee turned away from Melanie. "We've met," he said, giving Melanie the cold shoulder.

That's weird, Rebecca thought. But before she could say anything to Lee, the band launched into a slow number. Lee asked Rebecca to dance and she quickly accepted, glad to escape the dark mood brought on by Melanie's arrival.

On the dance floor Lee wasted no time in wrapping his arms around Rebecca and pulling her to close to his chest. Not that she minded. She had already given up on trying to remain in Cara's good graces. She knew Ross Peterson was out of her reach. She might as well have a good time with Lee.

She looked around her. Lee was definitely the cutest guy on the dance floor.

"So, tell me, how did Cara Worthington get involved in all of this? I can't see her risking a broken nail chasing a bunch of kids around an island."

Rebecca smiled wanly. "I had an application sent to her house as a joke. I guess her father got ahold of it somehow."

Lee laughed heartily. "He probably found it floating in the toilet where she had tossed it. She'll remember to flush twice next time."

"Sorry. I guess we're stuck with her for the summer."

Lee shrugged. "Nothing we can do about it now. I still doubt if she'll show up."

"Her dad's been threatening to make her work this summer because she's been running up so many credit card bills."

Lee laughed again. "He probably threatened to take her Beamer away."

They danced for a moment in silence. Rebecca felt warm and secure dancing with Lee. Rugged, handsome Lee. She conjured up an image of the two of them, alone, on a primitive island, swimming in a secluded cove . . .

He held her close to him. His hand pressed against the small of her back so there was no space between their bodies as they moved together rhythmically. She felt his heat through her clothes where their bodies touched. She was surprised how easy it was to let herself go in Lee's muscular arms. Her eyes closed and she breathed deeply, enjoying the smell of Lee's skin against her cheek. When she opened her eyes, she saw Ross Peterson back on the dance floor with his young date. But the feelings of jealousy were gone. Rebecca realized she no longer cared about Ross Peterson and his money. He was probably just another empty bucket, like the other rich guys Cara had introduced her to.

"I'm glad we're going to be together this summer," Lee said, as if reading her mind. "And Cara Worthington can go to hell."

He kissed her, and Rebecca thought she would melt.

She felt someone tapping her on the shoulder. It was Melanie. "May I cut in?" Rebecca stepped back, reluctantly, to give Melanie the dance. It had been such a tender moment she was sorry to see it pass.

"Get lost!" Lee growled at Melanie.

Melanie looked hurt, close to tears. "Lee!" Rebecca stared at Lee, open-mouthed. She looked at Melanie who was struggling not to cry. Lee continued to glare at her with burning eyes.

"I just wanted a dance, Lee," Melanie said softly. Her face quivered as her eyes filled with tears. Then Melanie lost it completely and broke down crying. She rushed out of the room.

Rebecca watched her go, then looked at Lee, baffled by his outburst. She hurried after Melanie but lost her in the crowded club which was packed with students celebrating with end-of-the-school-term parties.

She found Jenny Demos tending the snack bar. Jenny was the daughter of Jake Demos, the club's grouchy owner. She was an attractive woman in her mid twenties with medium length ash blond hair and two of the brightest, most violet eyes Rebecca had ever seen. Rebecca was friendly with Jenny. They had talked a lot back when Rebecca was considering whether to apply to the riding academy. Jenny didn't exactly give her advice, but Rebecca found that just talking to Jenny helped her make a decision.

"Jenny?"

Jenny, wiping down the counter, looked up at Rebecca and smiled, her bright eyes locking into Rebecca like twin laser beams. Rebecca felt something funny inside her brain, a tugging sensation. "Hi, Rebecca."

"Hi. Jenny, do you know a girl named Melanie . . . I already forgot her last name. Dark shaggy brown hair. Dresses crazy, wears big army boots—"

Jenny nodded. "I think I know the girl you mean. You just missed her. She ran out the door crying. Did you two have a fight?"

She'd never catch her now. "No, she and a friend of mine . . . do you know Lee Spinelli?"

"Yes."

"Well, the three of us are going to summer camp together. Actually, there's six of us. It's on a small island—a survival camp. So we had this get-together party. And then Lee met Melanie. Except I think he may have known her from before . . ."

She stopped when she realized she was rambling. The truth was, she really had no idea why Lee was mean to Melanie or why she had run away crying. Or why she was telling all this to Jenny.

"What's the name of this island?" Jenny asked innocently enough.

"Pig Island."

Jenny stopped what she was doing. She carefully folded

her bar rag and set it aside, wiped her hands on her apron. "Off the coast of Maine?"

"Yeah. Have you ever been there?"

"Oh, no," Jenny said, a little too quickly. "But I've . . . heard of it."

"Heard what?"

"Just some stories my dad told me."

"What kind of stories?"

Jenny seemed to shrug it off. "Just the usual ghost stories they love to tell in that part of the country. You know how superstitious New Englanders are. Don't forget, they used to burn witches in New England. What they *thought* were witches."

Rebecca cringed at the thought. To actually burn a person alive. Thank god she lived in a day and age when society was civilized.

"Oh, before you go . . ." Jenny dug around beneath the counter for a moment. "I have a little going away gift for you. If I can find it now." She pulled out a creaky drawer beneath the old mahogany bar and took something out.

Rebecca was a bit puzzled. She and Jenny had always been friendly to one another, but never close. A going away gift seemed a bit extravagant—especially a spur of the moment one.

Jenny handed Rebecca a tiny felt box, the type that usually held jewelry, before hurrying away to wait on a fresh herd of customers.

Rebecca opened the box.

Inside was a silver chain with a key attached.

She felt a shiver run up her spine.

The handle of the key was in the shape of a tiny skull.

Six

Lee arrived at the riding academy bright and early Monday morning to pick Rebecca up. He looked like anything but a survival camp counselor. He was wearing a bright red and yellow Hawaiian shirt, huge baggy shorts, black Converse hightops, no socks.

Rebecca was more sensibly dressed in brown, cuffed khaki shorts; a white, short sleeved polo shirt; and brown leather sandals. A blue and white striped crew neck cotton sweater was tied loosely around her neck.

Lee crammed another one of Rebecca's bags into the back of the station wagon. "You sure you brought enough stuff?" he said, wiping sweat from his brow.

The back of the station wagon was already laden down with gear even without Rebecca's contribution to the pile. She saw tents, sleeping bags, air mattresses, an ice chest, Coleman lanterns. A small canvas bag was stuffed behind the driver's seat, next to a black leather jacket.

"Are those your clothes?" she asked in disbelief, pointing to the canvas bag.

"Yeah," he said, looking at her quizzically.

"That's *all* you're taking?"

"Yeah. Bathing suit, cutoffs, T-shirts, jeans, sweatshirt." He gave her a sly smile. "I don't wear any underwear."

Rebecca raised her eyebrows at him as she climbed into the car. Lee slid in behind the wheel with a wolfish grin and turned the car motor over. The loaded-down station wagon bumped and clunked down the long riding academy driveway and away from the boring summer they might have had.

"You know, Lee, this is a *survival* camp," Rebecca said as they hit Old Wilson Highway. "It's not like we're going to be vegging out on a beach somewhere. You could have packed a few more things."

Lee seemed amused by her fears. "Hey, if these kids we're supposed to counsel can survive, we should be able to, right? I mean, how tough can it be?"

Rebecca looked at the postcard she held in her hand. The longer she looked at it, the darker and more foreboding the island seemed.

Lee glanced over at the postcard with a grin. "Yeah, I got one of those, too. Spooky, ain't it? Maybe we'll have to survive a bunch of ghosts or something."

She was reminded of what Jenny Demos had said about the island.

"I'll bet it's haunted," Lee was going on. "I *hope* it's haunted. I need a little excitement this summer."

"You're definitely weird, Lee."

"Maybe the guy who runs the camp, Fletcher, makes it look spooky on purpose. Part of the training to toughen us up psychologically."

Lee was full of ideas about what the camp would be like. It was the most upbeat she had seen him. Maybe getting away from Cooper Hollow was good therapy for him.

"You have the directions, navigator?" Lee asked.

The directions were on the back of the postcard. "Right here."

"That's good," Lee said. "Because I couldn't find this place on any map."

"It is pretty small," Rebecca admitted. "You could probably find it on the local maps. Not that we'll need to; the directions on the back of the postcard are pretty specific. Head for the expressway, and then go north . . . there's a little history of the island here. Did you read it?"

"I glanced at it. What's it say?"

"Years ago, when Edward Fletcher's grandfather was alive and running things, they used to hunt wild pigs on the island. Then Fletcher's father inherited the land and put an end to the killing—apparently the guy was a real animal lover—and turned the island into a game preserve.

"Edward Fletcher, the present owner, came up with the idea of turning the entire island into a survival summer camp to encourage young people to learn survival techniques, as well as self-confidence and all-around physical fitness."

Lee nodded. "Cool. It sounds like when I was a kid and me and my buddies used to play army in the woods. Are there still wild pigs on the island?"

She studied the postcard for a moment.

"One thing's for sure," Lee said. "It sure beats the hell out of spending another summer crawling around beneath a bunch of greasy cars at Zeke's Garage."

"It doesn't say here. But how dangerous can a pig be?"

"Don't the wild ones have horns or tusks or something like that?"

"I don't know," Rebecca said. "I've never seen a wild pig. Not counting some guys I've dated."

Lee chuckled. "Well, you don't have to worry about *either* kind of pig if you stick with me." Then he whipped a switchblade out of his pocket and flicked it open in one easy motion. "Show me a wild pig and I'll show you bacon for breakfast."

Rebecca's heart jumped into her throat as stared at the gleaming blade of the knife.

"A-yup," Lee said, imitating a New England accent as he

made stabbing motions in the air with the knife. "Oink, oink, oink!"

"Jesus," Rebecca muttered, shaking her head. "Will you please put that thing away? No wonder Cara thinks you're an animal."

"Coming from her, I take that as a compliment," Lee quipped, closing the knife blade with one hand.

"Well, I have a feeling you're going to get plenty of compliments this summer."

"I doubt it. There's just no way Cara Worthington is going to show up for a survival camp," Lee said, as he put the knife back into his pocket with the same easy motion with which he had removed it.

He looked over at Rebecca. "Hey, what's this?" he asked, pointing to her chest. When she looked down he flicked her nose. "Gets 'em every time," he laughed.

"Very funny," Rebecca said, rubbing her nose. She wondered if the whole summer was going to be like this. Lee seemed to be regressing rapidly.

"But seriously," Lee said, looking over at her again. "What's that thing around your neck?"

Rebecca reached up to her collarbone and felt the little skull key dangling from the thin, silver chain. She had forgotten all about it.

"It's a gift from Jenny Demos," she said. "You know, her father runs the Night Owl Club. I guess it's a sort of going away present." She removed the key from her neck and looked at it closely.

"Maybe it's to ward off evil spirits," she said, pushing the skull key toward him. "So watch yourself."

"Oh, I'm so scared," Lee said, recoiling in mock horror. "I don't know which is weirder: Jenny and Jake Demos, or that club they run."

"I like Jenny Demos."

"So do I, but I still think she's a little scary. Did you ever notice the way she looks at you sometimes? I don't know what she's thinking about, but there's something happening with those eyes of hers. Something . . . hypnotic. Totally weird."

Rebecca examined the pendant. The handle of the key, the skull part, appeared to be made of ivory. Or was it bone? She felt a sudden chill as the skull, briefly, seemed to glow.

"Hey—" Lee said, snapping her back to reality. "You want to see something *really* weird? Open up my bag behind the seat and take out that little book that's sitting on the top."

She reached back, tugged the small duffel bag onto her lap, and unzipped it. She found the book and pulled it out. The old, leather bound book she held in her hand was a manual on mantrapping and survival techniques in the wilderness. On the cover was an engraving of a skull. It looked a lot like her pendant.

Rebecca felt a chill run up her spine. "Where'd you get this?"

"That's what I was trying to tell you. Jenny Demos gave it to me! Is that weird or what?"

Rebecca flicked through the pages. "I guess."

"It's a pretty cool book, though," Lee said. "I've already read some of it."

Rebecca came to a very detailed illustration of a particularly lethal trap—the German Head Chopper—a booby trap designed to lop off the head of an unsuspecting trespasser.

She flicked through the manual, which was gross and fascinating at the same time. It was filled with descriptions of traps designed to maim or kill an enemy.

"Maybe we can rig a few of those if Cara Worthington actually does show up, which I still doubt," Lee said cheerfully. His expression darkened slightly. "Or Melanie Anderson—did you say north on the expressway?"

"Yeah." Rebecca closed the book to help Lee with the navigation. She pulled Lee's Rand McNally Road Atlas off the dashboard and opened it to the map of Maine.

Lee had been right. She couldn't find Pig Island anywhere on the map. She double checked the directions on the postcard. They were going the right way.

They drove on in silence for awhile. Rebecca wondered if thinking about Melanie had dampened Lee's mood. Rebecca searched for something to say. "So, you don't think Cara's going to show up?"

"I doubt it," Lee said.

"What about Melanie?"

A cold expression flashed over Lee's face. "I hope not."

"Lee, do you mind if I ask you why you were so rude to her last night?"

"Yes, I do," Lee snapped.

Rebecca felt annoyed, but let it pass. Maybe it was something too personal to talk about. Or maybe he would talk about it later when, and if, they got to know each other better. Still, the bad vibes she felt between Lee and Melanie made her a little nervous. She wondered if Melanie could be the girl Cara alluded to—the one who broke up with Lee. The one she said Lee beat up. But that wouldn't make sense. Why would Melanie want to dance with Lee after he hit her? Rebecca reminded herself that there was no reason to believe what Cara had told her. Still, she wished Lee would just tell her what happened instead of avoiding the topic.

Lee glanced over his shoulder at all the junk in the back of the car. "I'm surprised the front wheels of the car don't pop into the air with all the stuff we've got back there. Brian had a ton of new camping stuff and gave me all of it. He said his academy friend had enough for both of them."

Lee swerved into the passing lane to go around a slow moving truck.

"I just threw everything into the back of the wagon," Lee said. "I'm sure we'll find some use for it. You should see some of the stuff he's got—mosquito nets, about a dozen different bug sprays, he even has bear repellent. All this for a guy who's never even gone camping before."

"It makes you wonder why he was accepted to this camp."

Lee was quiet for a moment. "I've been thinking the same thing. Is Cara a good athlete, by the way? She moved around pretty good on the tennis court, I noticed that much."

"Cara's a *great* athlete," Rebecca said. "She was really into gymnastics until she suddenly grew breasts last summer. She even went to the Olympic trials one year."

Lee chuckled. "Yeah, I can see how big breasts would get in the way. They've already blotted out what little personality she has. Those and her dad's money."

"Why did you want to know if Cara was an athlete?"

"I was just wondering why Fletcher picked us. I thought maybe it was because of our athletic ability."

She took a chance. "What about Melanie? Is she a good athlete?"

Lee paused. "Yes, she is. She's very good. Over at Central High, in the next school district, she's the top ranked distance runner on the girl's track team. She's also a champion archer, believe it or not. She's won all sorts of trophies." He looked over at Rebecca. "Do you attend the riding academy on an athletic scholarship by any chance?"

"Yeah." Rebecca wondered if that made a difference to Lee.

"I thought as much."

"I also won a few swim meets at Cooper Hollow."

"You used to go to Cooper Hollow?"

"Yeah. You were a big deal on the football team until you quit."

Lee looked over at her long tanned legs. "I'm surprised I don't remember you."

"I was a year behind you."

"Not anymore," Lee muttered. A scowl formed on his face. "Thanks to Melanie Anderson . . ." Lee slammed on the brakes, nearly missing the entrance to the expressway. The tires squealed in protest as he made a sharp left. Rebecca was hurled against her door. Fortunately, the lock held.

The old wagon labored to pick up speed again as they rumbled down the off ramp. "What about Brian's friend?" Lee asked. "Know anything about him?"

"His name's Kevin something. A real big guy, like a weight lifter or football player or something." Rebecca looked Lee straight in the eye. "Lee, why did you give up football?"

Lee was quiet for a long time. "I'd like to blame it on my mom dying of cancer or my father becoming a drunk, but the truth is that I liked partying more than football. And the two don't mix. Not when you party as heavy as I did."

Rebecca looked over at Lee. He was no longer the playful child who flicked her nose a few minutes ago.

"There's a reason they call it dope," he said with a bitter edge to his voice. "Because there's nothing dopier than waking up every morning with your head feeling like a cracked egg. That's another reason I wanted to go to this camp. I want to try and get my life back together."

They drove on in silence for awhile. "Plus, I needed a summer job. I lost my job at the garage because of . . ." Lee drifted back into his melancholy mood.

One thing about driving with a person for over six hours, you get to know a lot about him, Rebecca discovered. There was no topic Lee was afraid to talk about, with the blaring exception of Melanie Anderson.

And the more she knew about Lee, the better she liked him. She knew he was a hothead at times; she had already seen him flash that temper of his. But the fire that burned inside of him also warmed his heart and gave him a brightness that became more obvious as the miles rolled by.

Lee hadn't played football his senior year because he was wrecked most of the time. He refused to blame it on his friends. He partied a lot because he enjoyed it. For awhile. Then, things began to backfire.

At least he still had a year of football eligibility left. He was determined to concentrate on making the team next fall when he returned for his senior year and get those college scouts interested in him again. He didn't want to be a loser like his friends. Or his father.

It was when his mother died that Lee's life went into a tailspin, from which he was just beginning to recover. He had started hanging out with tough guys—like the ones who gave them a lift from the country club. Guys who did drugs and drank and drove too fast to show how fearless they were. It didn't take Lee long to realize that these "fearless" guys were just trying to hide how scared they were—of life, of growing up, of failure.

Lee talked about his father, about how he wished his father would snap out of his funk. But Lee knew it was tougher for his old man than it was for him. He didn't blame his dad for drinking, but he sure wasn't going to follow in his footsteps.

Rebecca opened up, too, and told Lee things she never thought she'd tell anyone, much less a guy. She admitted she was poor and how it embarrassed her and she told him about her vague plans to marry some rich guy—she almost mentioned Ross Peterson by name, but caught herself just in time. She even admitted to being a virgin, although she wasn't sure why.

To her surprise, Lee didn't laugh.

Although, listening to herself, she realized she did sound

laughable with her Cinderella complex. She realized how immature she must sound, how muddled and poorly thought-out her plans were, like those of most girls her age, probably. But Lee didn't seem to judge her, or be put off by her naked ambition or her naive gullibility.

Maybe it was because he understood her. He was as poor as she was. And both their parents loved the bottle more than they did their own children.

They took Highway 1, the coastal route, and before long they could smell the salty, sea air. Rebecca tingled with anticipation as they neared the ferry landing for Pig Island. She realized that she had never been this excited about any summer before. Maybe it was the challenge of the survival camp that made her feel this way.

Or maybe it was Lee Spinelli's dark, handsome face.

Lee slipped a Beach Boys tape into the cassette player. He sang along with the tape for a moment before looking over at Rebecca, who was watching for the sign to the ferry.

"Remember when I kissed you Friday night, Rebecca?"

Rebecca smiled at the memory. "Yeah." She looked over at Lee. "Just before you yelled at Melanie."

Lee seemed slightly annoyed. Suddenly, he swerved sharply onto a smaller road. He had seen the sign to the ferry; she had missed it. They bumped down a road that grew narrower and dirtier. The sky before them began to grow dark as twilight turned to night and the moon fought to be seen.

Lee flicked on the car lights. "We must be near the ocean. I see fog up ahead."

They drove into the fog. "There's supposed to be a place to park down by the landing," Rebecca said, peering ahead as the fog grew thicker. "If we can find it."

"I hope there's no two way traffic on this road. I can barely see where I'm going." Lee flicked on the high beams, making the visibility even worse. He flicked back down to low beams and slowed the car to a crawl.

Lee suddenly braked, tossing Rebecca forward. The headlights of the station wagon played upon a small, handmade sign nailed to a pole: Pig Island Ferry.

He turned the station wagon into the parking lot adjacent to the launch slip and parked it beneath a large weeping willow tree. He shut the motor off and cut the lights. They saw no other cars.

"Do you think the others made it?" Lee asked.

"I don't know," Rebecca replied.

They sat in dark silence for a moment. Rebecca cracked her window, letting in fog and cool sea air. She heard a seagull cry high above them. She looked over at Lee and saw that he was looking back at her. Then he reached over and pulled her close, and a moment later his lips were on hers.

It wasn't as soft as the kiss the night before.

Or as short.

She liked this one better.

Lee broke the kiss, and smiled. He gazed at the chilly, foggy world outside the car window, then back at the dock. "Shall we explore?"

"Okay," she said, a little reluctant to leave the car and the pleasant feeling of warmth she felt from the tip of her toes to the top of her head. She grabbed her sweater from the back of the wagon and slipped it on. They clambered out of the car beneath the branches of the weeping willow tree.

As they slammed the car doors behind them, two dark figures rocketed out of the tree branches, screaming like banshees, and landed in front of them. Their attackers wore ski masks and dark clothing; they brandished wicked-looking machetes. Through the ski mask eye-holes, Rebecca saw twin sets of evil-looking eyes taking them in.

Then the figure closest to Rebecca sliced the air with the

machete. The blade hissed in a gleaming arc as the moonlight played off it.

Rebecca could easily imagine it cutting through her neck as if it were a stalk of celery.

She screamed as both figures rushed at them.

Seven

Lee pushed her aside and whipped out the switchblade. The blade extended with a menacing click and the two dark figures stopped dead in their tracks.

"Lighten up, cuz," Brian said, removing his mask.

Kevin did the same. "Just a little joke."

But Lee wasn't laughing. "I'll give you something to joke about!" He stuck the tip of the switchblade a fraction of an inch from Brian's nose. "Ever see the movie *Chinatown?*"

The argument abruptly ended when two bright car lights came flashing through the fog. Traveling far too fast for safety's sake, two thousand pounds of automotive steel came bearing down on them like a bat out of hell.

Lee grabbed Rebecca by the arm and pulled her back as the car nearly barreled into Brian and Kevin before screeching to a halt.

The car window slid down and Elton John's "The Bitch Is Back" came belting out through the stereo speakers and into the cool night air. "Is this the ferry to Pig Island?" Cara Worthington asked, sticking her head through the open window.

Brian and Kevin still had their machetes gripped tightly in their hands and neither was very happy about nearly being run down. Rebecca stepped into Cara's line of vision, perhaps to save her from a bloody fate.

"Oh. Hello," Cara said frostily.

"I see you made it." Rebecca tried to sound friendly, even though she had almost been scared to death twice in the past few minutes, first by the boys, then by Cara's erratic driving.

"Yeah," Cara grumbled. "It was either a summer job or daddy cuts my allowance. I hope it's worth it. I can't believe I even found this place. Lucky I picked up Melanie hitchhiking or we wouldn't be here. My sense of direction is—"

"You almost ran us over you idiot!" Brian bellowed.

"Hey! Watch your mouth, junior!" Cara snapped back.

Rebecca peeked into the car and saw Melanie. When she looked up she saw in the glare of Cara's headlights a van parked at the far end of the parking lot.

"You want I should rough her up, Bri?" Kevin asked. It was hard to tell if he was kidding or not.

"Hey, gimme a break, huh?" Cara's eyes took in Kevin. "A big butt like yours is hard to miss, okay?"

Brian and Kevin approached her car, the machetes swinging menacingly at their sides. Cara's window quickly slid back up at the same time the door locks snapped shut.

Rebecca heard a motor chugging in the distance. "Do you hear that?" she asked Lee.

"I think our ride might be here," Lee said, closing the blade of his knife against his thigh and slipping it back into his pocket. "Let's go check it out."

He took her hand and without a word to the others they walked down to the launch slip. At the end of the dock they found a boat moored. An old man appeared on the deck.

"Mr. Fletcher?" Lee said, uncertainly.

"No, can't say that I am," said the man.

Rebecca checked the old guy out. He went well with the fog. He was as thin as a wisp and as pale as a ghost. His eyes looked glazed and out of focus, and his nose, which was considerable, was veined with thin red streaks, the ruptured capillaries of an alcoholic.

The rest of his face resembled a stewed prune. He was a living portrait of an old sailor on his last sea legs, and his boat couldn't be far behind. It looked too small to be a ferry, and too dilapidated to be safe.

"Can you tell us what time the ferry to Pig Island arrives?" Rebecca asked.

"This *is* the ferry."

"*This* is the ferry?" Lee asked, skeptical.

"That's right, sonny. My name's Martin. Are the others here yet?"

"Yeah," Lee said.

"Then let's get your gear loaded on and make way. Mr. Fletcher doesn't like to be kept waiting."

Rebecca and Lee went to fetch the others, who were still arguing heatedly through the closed window of the car. Informed that their ferry was here, the argument abruptly ended.

They collected their stuff and made their way back to the launch slip. Lee jumped down into the boat to help load.

"I don't think Cara and Melanie even brought any camping gear," Lee said, taking hold of a bag Rebecca handed to him and tossing it to the deck of the boat. Martin was somewhere down below, fiddling with the boat engine.

"She probably planned to buy it when she got here."

"It's lucky I brought along some extra stuff. Unless you want to share a tent with them."

"No thanks," Rebecca said, making a face. She had a feeling her friendship with Cara was pretty much over, what there had been of it. "Are you mad that Melanie's here?"

Lee shrugged. "I pretty much expected it. She must've found out what my plans for the summer were from one of my friends and decided to do the same."

Rebecca was about to ask Lee why Melanie would follow him anywhere, when Brian and Kevin suddenly appeared out of the fog, laden down with supplies. Kevin carried the bulk of it like a loyal pack mule. Cara and Melanie lingered nearby, within earshot. She decided to wait for a more opportune time to question Lee about Melanie.

Lee helped Brian and Kevin load their gear into the boat, which was sinking lower and lower into the water. Cara watched the small boat rocking uneasily as the gear was stowed away. Gray-green water lapped at the pilings and the boat rocked gently in the water as they finished their task. Nearby, a sea gull clamored in the sand, pecking at a dead crab. A few minutes later, Martin appeared from below, ordered them all aboard, and cast off.

The launch pulled away from the slip, its engine roaring loudly. As they made their way out to sea, the wind whipped up the ocean, making it choppy.

Rebecca leaned against the cabin wall, next to Lee, who was looking out at the ocean. He had slipped on a gray, hooded Champion sweatshirt to protect himself from the cool, wet spray of the ocean.

The hood was pulled tightly about his head, throwing his face into a shadow. Over this he had put on his black leather jacket. The outfit gave him the appearance of a strange kind of sea phantom.

The boat hit a swell and Rebecca lurched forward, off balance. Lee caught her arm and held her. He pushed her wet hair back with his hand as she folded into him and looked out to the ocean, a warm smile on her face.

Suddenly Melanie came into her field of vision, a bitter smile frozen upon her face. Rebecca lost sight of her when they drifted into a fog bank.

She leaned closer into Lee. He gave her a soft kiss on her

forehead. She felt excited and nervous at the same time, to be heading off to a mysterious island with him.

At the Cooper Hollow Riding Academy, where Rebecca had lived during the school term, her activities were always closely supervised. From morning until night, adult monitors were in every dormitory wing to enforce curfew and other rigid rules.

She had attended the Cooper Riding Academy for only one term. Somewhere between Cooper Hollow and Pig Island, she realized just how much she hated it.

And now she was free.

With a strange, but attractive, boy. The fact that no one she knew would approve of Lee Spinelli only heightened her excitement.

The feeling was exhilarating.

Now was the time to *live*. Before she had to go back to rigid atmosphere of the riding academy. If she did go back. Feeling the warmth and power of Lee's muscular arms, even through his sweatshirt and leather jacket, gave her second thoughts. There was no Lee at the riding academy.

There were no boys *whatsoever* at the Cooper Hollow Riding Academy. The more she thought about it, the more enticing the idea of returning to Cooper Hollow High seemed to her. There, she could watch Lee Spinelli dazzle the college recruiters with long touchdown runs.

About twenty minutes later, in the distance, through the fog, she could make out the vague outline of a mass of land.

Pig Island.

An uneasy feeling seeped into pit of her stomach. What was causing it? The rough ride across the open sea to the island? Her rift with Cara? The mysterious Melanie? Her indecision about returning to school and what the future might hold for her back at Cooper Hollow?

Pig Island drew closer.

THE KILLING GAME

She felt a tickling sensation on her chest. She looked down at the little skull hanging from her neck.

It seemed to be glowing.

Eight

"Sorry about the bumpy ride," Martin said, pulling into a small landing dock.

He shut down the smoking boat engine and tied up to a dock that wasn't in much better shape than the boat moored to it. They were all drenched, and Rebecca was a little woozy with seasickness. The others didn't look too well either.

It hadn't been a pleasant ride. The little boat had sprung numerous leaks on the ride over and Martin had dashed about frantically patching things up and pumping out water.

"The water's unusually choppy tonight," Martin said, as if apologizing for the sea.

"I think I may have to puke," Cara grumbled to no one in particular, climbing out of the boat. Her bright red hair had grown incredibly frizzy in the salty ocean air.

The others followed her onto the shore. Lee tugged off his hood and wiped the cold ocean sea spray from his face with the sleeve of his sweatshirt. Rebecca stood near him, shivering. He put his arms around her and rubbed her until she stopped shaking.

Rebecca noticed Melanie staring icily at them and looked away.

"Where's Kevin?" Lee asked Brian.

"Up by the bow of the boat. We had a few beers on the ride down and I think the boat ride upset his delicate little tummy."

THE KILLING GAME

Brian looked a little green in the face himself.

Lee just shook his head. "Big tough, academy guys," he said to Rebecca under his breath.

Martin started tossing their gear onto the dock as if he were in a hurry to leave.

"I'm really soaked," Cara complained, running her hand through her wet, frizzy hair.

"So am I," Melanie said, pulling her suitcase from the pile and dragging it to the end of the dock. From her bag she pulled out a thick, black fisherman's sweater, glanced briefly over her shoulder—at Lee, Rebecca thought—before slipping out of her wet sweatshirt and unhooking her bra. She let both items fall to the ground.

A shaky Kevin stepped out of the boat and stared with wide eyes as Melanie finished her little strip tease. Bright pink panties were briefly visible before her oversized sweater fell over them. Then she slipped into a pair of baggy lime green parachute pants.

"She sure ain't shy, is she?" Kevin asked, wiping his lips with the back of his hand.

"She sure ain't," Brian agreed, tucking his own eyes back into his head.

Rebecca glanced at Lee, who was trying not to look at Melanie, and felt a pang of jealousy. Melanie finished dressing and wandered off into the night.

Cara shrugged, grabbed a bag, and went to look for a suitable place to change. Rebecca, also wet and cold, grabbed one of her bags and walked to the edge of the woods.

She scanned the area, found a suitable bush and slipped behind it. She wasn't nearly as bold as Melanie. She opened her bag and pulled out some dry clothes. She tugged on a pair of faded denim jeans and dry socks, and pulled her sneakers back on.

She was slipping into a dry sweater when she heard a twig

snap at the edge of the woods. Right behind her. She spun around and saw an eye—*one* eye—gleaming back at her through the darkness.

Before she could cry out, the eye had vanished.

Then someone grabbed her from behind.

Nine

She screamed and struggled against the strong arms that held her tightly by the shoulders.

"Hey, easy there." Lee laughed. "Sorry, I didn't mean to scare you. I was afraid you might have wandered off and gotten lost." Brian and Kevin came running over.

"What was that?" Brian asked excitedly. "Who screamed?"

Cara also hurried over, buttoning up an oversized black and red wool flannel shirt. "What's all the excitement. Did someone scream?"

"It's nothing. Everything's cool," Lee said. "I just scared Rebecca—"

"There was someone—some*thing*—in the woods staring at me," Rebecca said.

A hush fell over the group.

"What do you mean . . . *something?*" Cara asked skeptically.

"It had only *one* eye," Rebecca said nervously.

They all laughed loudly, breaking the tension for the moment.

Rebecca blushed red with a mixture of anger and embarrassment.

"I'm sorry, Rebecca," Lee said, still a little giggly. "But are you sure you're not just seeing bogey men in the dark—"

"I'm sure," Rebecca snapped back, her eyes still scanning

the edge of the wood, her heart still hammering inside her chest. "It was staring right at me."

"Where was this one-eyed monster?" Kevin asked smirking.

Rebecca pointed to where she had seen the eye.

Kevin walked to the edge of the woods, looked around a little, came back. "Well, I don't see nothing," he said, scratching his short, bristly hair with big, fat stubby fingers. "Probably just a raccoon or something."

"A one-eyed raccoon?" Rebecca asked, in disbelief.

"Could've lost it in a fight," Kevin said. "I once played in a football game against Cooper Hollow where this guy nearly got his eye gouged out."

"I remember that game," Brian said proudly.

"So do I." Lee looked directly at Kevin. "Didn't they accuse *you* of doing it?"

"It was a big pileup. No one could prove anything," Kevin asserted, looking at Lee closely for the first time. "What did you say your name was?"

"I didn't."

"It's Spinelli," Brian said. "I told you before. My cousin, Lee Spinelli."

"You look different with your helmet off," Kevin said.

"You don't," Lee replied.

"So where's this Fletcher guy, anyway?" Cara asked. "Isn't he supposed to meet us here? I'm hungry."

"He didn't say anything about meeting us," Brian said. "All it said on the back of the postcard was to catch the ferry over here. But I think we should wait until he comes to get us."

Melanie suddenly appeared out of the night. "It's beautiful down by the beach. The coast line stretches forever and I think the fog is lifting." She looked directly at Lee. "Would anyone like to go for a walk with me? Do a little exploring?"

Lee looked away.

"I think maybe we should just stay here until Mr. Fletcher or someone comes to get us," Brian said again.

"What's the matter, Brian?" Cara asked. "Afraid of the dark?" Brian made a face. Cara looked at Melanie. "I'll go with you."

"Don't let the bogey man get you," Brian said, watching them go. He walked back toward the dock, followed by Kevin.

Rebecca watched them disappear into the darkness. She could vaguely see the old wooden dock now. The fog *was* breaking up, she noted with relief. The island was spooky enough as it was without looking like a set from a *Friday the 13th* movie.

She walked to the water's edge. The white-capped ocean sparkled brightly as the light from a pale yellow crescent moon broke through the haze. A million twinkling stars dotted the sky above them. They listened for a moment to the waves crashing rhythmically on the nearby beach. It had a hypnotic effect on Rebecca and she realized she was very tired.

"It really is beautiful," she said, and Lee murmured his agreement. The beach stretched away from them for quite a distance before disappearing around a bend.

"Lee?"

"Yeah?"

"Never mind." Rebecca was conscious of Lee staring at her, but his gaze was warm.

"No, really," Lee persisted. "What were you going to say?"

"Oh, I don't know. You'll just think I'm overreacting, but I know I saw that eye. And it made me think about this camp in a different way. I mean, don't you think it's strange that all the counselors are from our town?"

"Well, yeah, it is a little weird. There must be plenty of teenagers in Maine who could use the kind of money that Fletcher is paying."

"Exactly. So why did he have to import us all the way from Cooper Hollow? Won't the local kids work for him? Jenny Demos said the island could be haunted."

"Yeah, by one-eyed monsters," Lee joked. Rebecca punched Lee playfully on the shoulder. "Seriously, though," Lee continued, "I don't know why he'd hire us from so far away. Let's ask him if—I mean when—we meet him."

Rebecca was reassured by Lee's matter-of-fact response, and relieved that he hadn't made fun of her for being so suspicious. This was such a romantic spot. She wondered if Lee was thinking the same thing, but when she turned her head back to him, she noticed Lee gazing up into the woods. "See something?" she asked.

"A trail."

She looked into the woods and saw it, too, a narrow trail winding through tall pine trees and up a sloping hill. "Where do you think it goes?"

"Probably to Fletcher's house."

Just then they heard Martin's boat engine roar to life. "Maybe Martin knows." Rebecca hurried to the end of the dock. Martin was already casting off by the time she reached him.

"Excuse me? Martin? Can you tell us how to get to Mr. Fletcher's house?"

Martin said nothing as he pulled the launch quickly away from the dock.

"Mr. Martin!" she call loudly.

But the launch was already making its way out to sea, the engine grinding noisily. Maybe he hadn't heard her.

"What did Martin say?" Lee asked when she returned.

"Ah . . . nothing. He left before I had a chance to ask to him."

"Hmmm . . ." Lee looked up at the narrow trail. "Well, maybe we should check it out anyway."

"I—I don't know," Rebecca replied haltingly, recalling the eye that had watched her. "There *was* something in the woods . . ."

"Of course there was something in the woods. They're called *animals*. Ever hear of them?" Rebecca was a little put off by Lee's sarcasm. "Come on," he coaxed. "It's a small island. What could happen?"

Before she could answer, Lee turned and strode up the dock. "Hey! You guys want to go exploring?" She could hear him shouting to Brian and Kevin, who sat at the end of the dock on a large ice chest, two open cans of beer in their hands.

Brian came reluctantly off the ice chest. "Why? What's up?"

Lee nodded to the trail. "Rebecca and I are thinking of taking a hike up that trail."

"Now? In the middle of the night?" Brian asked, his eyes wide.

"Yeah. Now. To see if Fletcher's home. You wanna come along?"

Brian shot a fearful glance up the hill. "I don't know . . ." He glanced back at the beach. "What about the girls? We can't just walk off and leave them."

Lee gave his cousin a faint smile. "Well, you can stay with the girls if you want, cuz, but Rebecca and I are going up that hill."

"We are?" Rebecca said. She wasn't enthusiastic about the idea.

Lee gave Rebecca a challenging look. "Coming with me? Or do you want to stay here with these guys?"

Rebecca gave it some thought, but not much. "Ah . . . let me just see if I can find the girls, first." She jogged down to the beach and looked up and down the shoreline.

The beach was deserted.

"Cara!" she shouted. "Melanie!"

Faintly in the distance, she heard a cry for help.

She strained her ears to hear more.

But only a night bird answered her.

That's all it had been. A bird. A creature in the woods. It wasn't a scream and all.

"Cara!" she shouted at the top of her lungs. "Melanie!"

The wind whipped her words out to sea.

She noted, with some surprise, that she was nervously fingering the little skull key Jenny Demos had given her.

A few more calls brought no response. She turned around and jogged back the way she had come.

"Find them?" Lee inquired as she rejoined the group.

Rebecca shook her head. "They just disappeared."

"Oooooooooo!" Kevin wailed, as if on cue. He took a hit of beer and belched loudly.

"Knock it off!" Lee snapped. "Or I'll give you something to 'ooo' about."

Kevin put down his beer, walked over to Lee, and grabbed him roughly by the collar of his leather jacket. Lee slapped his hand away. Rebecca could see Lee reaching for his knife.

The still of the night air was broken by a high, piercing shriek.

"What the hell was that?" Brian asked, swallowing hard. "Some kind of bird?"

"I don't know, Bri, but it didn't sound like any bird I've ever heard before," Kevin said, his eyes scanning the woods, then up into the star-bright sky.

"Sounded like a bat," Lee said, looking up the hill. "Well, I'm going for a walk. You chickens can stay here and keep scaring each other to death if you want." Lee turned and strode confidently toward the trail that twisted into the black woods.

"Academy fears nothing," Brian said, his voice full of bravado. Suddenly the wind picked up and whistled through the trees, making an eerie sound. "Kevin—take the point!"

"After you," Lee said, as Kevin jogged past him.

"What about our stuff?" Rebecca asked when Brian hurried off to catch Kevin, who was now double-timing it up the hill.

"I wouldn't worry about it. I don't think there's anyone else on this island to steal it."

They walked up the path, into the shadows of large pine trees. Rebecca thought she heard a rustling behind every bush, a creature in every tree, as the trail led deeper into the woods.

The skull key, gently resting against the cool skin of her chest, seemed to be vibrating now.

"Lee?" she called.

He was walking a few feet ahead of her on the narrow path and she could barely see him in his black leather jacket. He stopped and turned to face her.

"Yeah?"

His voice didn't sound as confident as it had back down on the beach.

"I'm scared," she whispered.

Lee chuckled and slipped his arm around her. "So am I," he whispered in her ear. Then he kissed her earlobe, making Rebecca giggle. For a moment she forgot her fear, but it returned with her next breath.

"Why do you think Fletcher wasn't at the dock to meet us?"

"I don't know," Lee said. "Maybe he just forgot about us."

"I thought you and Kevin were going to get in a fight back there."

"I remember him from playing football. The dirtiest player on the field."

"You don't think he's going start something, do you?"

They came to a small clearing. "Never mind Kevin. Why don't you and I start a little something?" Lee stopped and wrapped his arms around her. His hands slipped low and brushed the back pockets of her jeans.

He kissed her long and deep. She returned the kiss, wrapping her arms around him. She could smell the soft leather of his jacket. Like an animal's skin. She tilted her head back and went limp in his arms, giving herself to his passionate kiss.

The mood was abruptly broken when a terrified scream ripped through the night air.

Ten

Brian came barreling back down the trail, his arms churning at his side. He would have shot right past if Lee hadn't grabbed him as he ran by, practically yanking him off his feet.

"What happened up there?" Lee asked. "Where's Kevin?"

Brian was gasping for air. "Something got him!"

"What?" Lee demanded. Brian struggled to free himself. Lee slapped him hard in the face. "Brian, chill out man! What got Kevin?"

"I don't know, man," Brian said, rubbing his bright pink cheek, calming down a little. "But it lifted him right up into the air. He never had a chance."

Then they all heard it.

A scream for help.

Kevin's scream.

Lee shot a fearful glance up the path. "We've got to go up there and help him!"

"Not me!" Brian said, growing panicky again, trying to squirm out of Lee's grasp. "I'm getting on that boat and getting the hell out of here!"

"There is no boat," Rebecca said. "Martin left the island."

Kevin's scream ripped through the night again.

"What about your pal up there?" Lee asked.

"What about him?"

Lee roughly pushed Brian away. "Fearless academy man,"

he muttered. He looked at Rebecca. "I'm going to help Kevin. Maybe you and Brian should go find the girls. We should all stick together until we find out what's going on."

Rebecca was insulted. "I'm going with you!"

Lee hesitated, then shrugged. Without another word he tore up the path with Rebecca close at his heels. Rebecca heard Brian tagging along behind them, either too afraid to go off by himself to search for the girls, or perhaps to help them if they needed him after all.

They made their way up the curving path, which was thickly covered with dead, brownish pine needles, until they bumped into Kevin.

Literally.

He was dangling upside down, one foot caught in a snare, struggling frantically to free himself. The snare was attached to a tree branch that had functioned as spring pole and catapulted him into the air.

Kevin's face had turned a beet red. "Are you guys going to stand around gawking or are you going to get me out of this thing!"

"No one move," Lee ordered, his eyes scanning the ground in front of them. "We might be walking into another trap."

Then they all froze as slow laughter erupted from directly behind them. They turned around quickly and saw a man with long white hair pulled back into a ponytail framing a tanned, leathery face. He carried a hunting rifle, and leaned against the weapon as if it were a cane. His face, half in shadow, seemed frozen in a scowl.

Rebecca did a double take—the man seemed to have appeared out of nowhere. The woods on both sides of the path were thick and she hadn't heard so much as a twig snap or a leaf rustle. She wondered if he were some kind of ghost who could move silently through objects.

Then this ghost spoke, in a very human voice. "When in

THE KILLING GAME 85

enemy territory, especially in a strange land at night, you must exercise extreme caution. Unlike this gentleman," the man said, pointing to Kevin.

He stepped out of the shadows and they got a better look at him. He was a tall, barrel-chested man, wearing a brown khaki safari jacket over baggy brown, chino pants, and black and green jungle boots. Hanging from a thick, brown leather ammunition belt was a holstered pistol and long, sheathed knife.

Kevin pointed at Lee. "It was his idea. The rest of us wanted to stay and wait for someone to come and get us."

The stranger smiled indulgently at Kevin. "But it is *you* who got caught in the trap."

The man looked at each teenager in turn and said in a gruff voice, "Good evening." His eyes rested on Lee. "That was very astute of you, Lee, to anticipate another trap. Have you trapped man before?"

"Absolutely, sir," Lee said with a straight face. "I started off with squirrels before working my way up to human beings."

The man laughed heartily. "Please accept my apologies for this little demonstration," he said, his tone softening a little. "But, as they say, a picture is worth a thousand words." He slid the hunting knife from its sheath and cut the rope holding Kevin. Kevin fell to the ground with a painful thump.

"With a little bit of rope, a sharp knife, and the surrounding environment, one can easily incapacitate an enemy. Allow me to introduce myself. I am Edward Fletcher. The owner of this little island."

He shook each of their hands in turn, looking into each face for several long moments, as if he were sizing them up.

He came to Rebecca last. He already knew her name. He

knew all their names. Rebecca remembered he had asked for detailed physical descriptions of each of them. Apparently, he had done his homework.

He locked her into his gaze, his large rough hand smothering hers. His eyes were blue, penetrating, and bloodshot. He gave her the chills.

"We still have two more friends down by the beach," Rebecca said, finally disentangling her hand from his.

He gave her a faint smile. "Cara Worthington and Melanie Anderson. They're already back at the house." He looked at the others. "If you all will follow me, you will find food and refreshment at the house. Don't worry about your gear; we'll pick it up tomorrow."

They followed Fletcher up the hill, Lee and Rebecca lagging behind a little.

"Do you think this guy's on the level?" Lee asked.

Rebecca shrugged. "He does seem a little eccentric, but I guess we should have expected that. Living on this island and the survival camp and all. How'd you know to expect another trap, by the way?"

"I read about it in that survival book Jenny Demos gave me. Most people never expect a second trap right after the first one, so they let their guard down."

At the top of the hill they reached a white-washed house, gleaming in the pale moonlight. It was an enormous, two-storied house—more like a small fort, really—with an odd, sloping, red shingled roof and tall, smooth walls.

The house sat on the highest point of the island. Now that the fog had cleared they could see more of the moonlit bay on the southwest tip of the island. The dock where they had landed, far down below, looked like a tiny toy.

Fletcher led them up a cobbled walk and straight to a tall, wooden double door that formed the entrance. The keyhole in the door was in the shape of a leering wolf head. It seemed majestic and mysterious at the same time.

And more than a little foreboding.

Fletcher pulled an old brass key from a large pocket of his safari jacket and fit it into the keyhole.

Suddenly, the skull around Rebecca's neck felt hot. She stifled a gasp of surprise and resisted the temptation to rip it off. As quickly as it had come, the pain went away.

Fletcher pushed open the thick wooden door. They entered the house and stepped into a large hall.

Rebecca saw that Cara and Melanie were already seated at a long wooden table, eating. Fletcher pointed to the banquet table and invited them all to sit down and eat. Then he limped across the spacious banquet hall floor, past the grizzly bear rug, toward a hallway at the far end of the room.

The group eagerly made their way to the banquet table, but stopped, slightly startled, at the sight of a gargantuan roasted pig, a bright red apple sticking out of its mouth beneath the huge snout.

A long, sharp carving knife was thrust into the pig. A serving tray next to it held carved slices of its flank. There was also fruit and soft drinks and a large wooden bowl full of fresh salad.

"Wow," Lee said. "I never saw the whole pig cooked like that."

"It is kind of gross looking," Rebecca admitted.

"Well, it tastes good," Cara said, chewing on a mouthful of food. She eagerly speared another slice of pork and dropped it on her plate.

As she ate, Rebecca studied the room. The floor was made of stone. An enormous bear rug lay in the middle. The huge room was paneled in dark mahogany; exposed wooden beams ran along the ceiling. All the furniture was heavy and sturdy looking, made of thick, dark wood and heavy leather cushions.

But what really held Rebecca's attention were the heads of dead animals lined along the mahogany paneled walls: wolf, bear, deer, moose, some birds. It was as if they were still alive, the rest of their bodies obscured behind the wood walls. Rebecca swallowed hard.

This isn't a summer camp, she thought. It's a *hunting lodge*.

"Kev, why don't you run back down that hill and bring us up a few beers," Brian suggested.

"No way, man," Kevin said. "Who knows how many traps that guy's got set out there?"

Brian shrugged, then sliced off a piece of pig flank and bit into it. He chewed for a moment. "Not bad," he said, smacking his lips. "Fresh. Very fresh."

"You won't believe what happened to us," Cara said, between mouthfuls of food. "Me and Melanie went for a walk down the beach, and we must've been about a hundred yards or so from the dock, when we fell into this giant sand pit."

"I kept expecting some mutant, radioactive crab to come crawling along and gobble us up," Melanie said.

"But then we hear this laughter. We look up and see this Fletcher guy looking down at us like we're some bugs caught in a trap," Cara said.

"And he's laughing like it's the funniest thing in the world," Melanie said.

"Didn't you guys hear us calling for help?" Cara asked, forking salad from a large wooden bowl onto her plate. "I was yelling my head off."

"Talk about yelling one's head off, wait until Kev tells you what happened to him" Brian said. "Fortunately, I was there to rescue him."

"Right, cuz," Lee muttered. "You lie worse than that bear rug over there."

Rebecca's eyes were scanning the wall. "What's with all these animal heads?"

Lee bit into an apple. "Wasn't Fletch's grandfather a hunter or something? These must be his trophies."

As they ate, Brian told Cara and Melanie his version of what happened to Kevin. He was careful not to look at Rebecca or Lee, who knew he was revising what really happened to fit his inflated self-image.

About half an hour later, just as Brian was finishing up his story, they heard Fletcher clear his throat. Rebecca hadn't heard him reenter the room, and the others seemed as startled as she was by his sudden appearance.

Fletcher leaned on his hunting rifle as he addressed the group. "I'd like to welcome you all to Pig Island. As you may know Pig Island was once a hunting ground until my father turned it into a game preserve. When father died earlier this year in an unfortunate boating accident, I returned from the Amazon where I had been working as a . . . tour guide . . . and decided to turn the island into a survival camp.

"This is the first year of the survival camp, and I am proud to announce that you six lucky young people have been especially chosen to be its initial camp counselors. Congratulations to all of you."

Cara wasn't impressed. "You mean, we're the first to *ever* do this?"

"That's what the man said," Lee said.

"So in other words we're like . . . like, ah . . ." Cara's eyes fell upon the roast pig, its dead eyes staring blankly into space ". . . like a bunch of guinea pigs."

Fletcher gave her a bemused smile. "In a way, yes, but

I'm sure you'll find your stay on the island quite entertaining."

"What about the others?" Lee asked. "When do they get here?"

"The senior counselors will arrive later this week with the rest of the campers. During your first week on the island I will teach you a few tricks about surviving in the wilderness."

Rebecca let her gaze wander around the room. She wondered how the others were reacting to this announcement.

Lee looked slightly puzzled.

The Academy boys were nodding eagerly.

Cara had a dubious look on her face.

And Melanie was staring back at her.

Rebecca quickly turned her attention back to Mr. Fletcher. "Sir, are there . . . like . . . still wild animals on the island and stuff?"

Fletcher chuckled lightly. "You may run into a wild boar or two. If you do, stay away from them. Their tusks are small but razor sharp. And, like most pigs, they have a foul temperament."

Rebecca's eyes fell upon the roasted pig on the banquet hall table. Fresh meat. "Are we going to have to hunt these animals? Because I don't think I could kill something."

"You may surprise yourself with abilities you did not realize you possessed," Fletcher said. "But it isn't only the animals on the island that you will be hunting."

A strange glint came into his eyes.

"You will also be hunting *each other*."

Eleven

"Excuse me? What do you mean hunting each other?" Cara asked.

Fletcher's eyes locked into Cara. "Survival in the world of the future may well some day return to the most primitive of confrontations—human versus human. One mad terrorist armed with a nuclear weapon could level a modern city and turn it into a concrete jungle. One trident submarine commanded by a skipper gone mad could destroy over *two hundred* cities."

Fletcher's lips quivered slightly as his eyes took in the rest of them. "When the smoke has cleared from the rubble, who will get that can of food, that bottle of uncontaminated water, that packet of powered milk, that may well mean the difference between life and death? *Your* life or *your* death!"

He said it with such fervor, the knuckles of the hand gripping the rifle barrel had turned white. "This guy's been watching too many *Mad Max* movies," Lee whispered to Rebecca.

Fletcher paused and took a moment to compose himself. He wiped away a bead of sweat that had formed on his upper lip. "Tomorrow, we will begin day one of your training. Tonight you will sleep here in the lodge, but tomorrow night, and every night after that, you will sleep in the wild. Are there any questions?"

Cara still looked puzzled. Rebecca wondered how much of this was seeping into Cara's privileged head. Cara raised her hand as if she were still in class, and waited for Mr. Fletcher to acknowledge her, which he did with a nod of his head. "Uh, do you mean, like . . . sleep outside?"

"Yes."

"In the cold?"

"Yes."

Cara patted at her wild frizzy hair, as if to tame it. "What if you didn't bring a tent? I guess you'd have to sleep here in the lodge, right?"

"I brought a few extras, Mr. Fletcher," Lee said.

"Excellent, Lee. Thank you. So . . . if there are no further questions I will show you to your rooms. Get a good night's sleep, we have a lot to do tomorrow."

At dawn they were brusquely awakened by Fletcher and served a quick breakfast, after which they returned to the dock to pick up their gear. From there, Fletcher led them to a clearing in the woods not far from the main trail that led up the hill to the house.

The clearing was little more than a rough circle of dirt with an outhouse and a small shower, but it was there that they made camp.

Fletcher showed them how to set the camp up. Lee had brought three tents. He gave one to Rebecca and the other to Cara. Fletcher had a spare tent for Melanie. Brian and Kevin shared a tent that was bigger than all their tents put together.

When camp was set up, Fletcher took them into the woods and demonstrated how to set a snare trap, the same type of trap that had caught Kevin the night before.

"This is one of the easiest traps to make, but still highly

effective," Fletcher explained as he bent back a small sapling tree with one hand.

"When setting a snare, bear in mind the game you wish to catch. In order to catch, let's say, a four pound rabbit, you may not need an extreme amount of pressure on your spring pole."

He bent the sapling even further back, his bicep muscle bulging from the exertion. For an older guy, he looked pretty strong. Rebecca could easily imagine him living in a distant jungle. "But for heavier game—such as a human—heavier pressure on the spring pole must be supplied."

He let go of the sapling and the young tree whooshed through the air with such force that it blew off Melanie's dark wool ski cap.

Such as a human. The thought of trapping a fellow human being sent a chill up Rebecca's spine.

"Excuse me," Cara said, obviously bored with the snare setting demonstration. "Is all this really necessary? I mean, can't we just go to the store and buy a rabbit or something."

Fletcher chuckled. "The nearest grocery store is on the mainland. If you want to eat, you'll have to catch your dinner."

Cara paled. "You're kidding."

"Do we get to slaughter what we catch?" Brian asked eagerly.

"You will," Fletcher said, giving Brian a benevolent smile. "And I will show you how to do that as well."

"What if you don't eat meat?" Cara asked.

"You eat meat," Brian cracked.

Cara made a face at Brian. "Shut up, Brian. I'm not talking about cocktail sausages."

"There's a vegetable garden and a blueberry patch behind the house," Fletcher continued. "You may help your selves. The stream you passed is your source of fresh water. But I assure you, if you enjoy meat, my traps are very effective."

He fixed them all with an enigmatic gaze. "And I always catch my prey."

A shadow fell across Rebecca's face. She looked up and saw a hawk glide swiftly across the pale blue sky before disappearing into a cluster of pine trees.

They spent the rest of the day making and setting their traps. There was a lot of trial and error, but by the end of the day, with Fletcher's expert instruction, they had snared several rabbits and even an armadillo, which they let go.

They would eat well their first night in the wild.

On the second day of training, they hiked over most of the island, with the exception of the North Cliff, and learned more survival techniques.

Fletcher spoke about Darwin's principle of survival of the fittest. "Many of today's problems," he lectured, "are the result of our society's predilection for pampering the weak." Fletcher spat the word "weak" as if it were a personal affront that beings he considered inferior were allowed to live at all. "My father, for example, was a weak man—hard to believe he was the only son of such a great hunter as my grandfather. But instead of toughening him up, my grandfather allowed my father's weakness to fester. My father was afraid to kill animals, and hid his fear behind the mask of a conservationist." Fletcher seemed oblivious to the counselors he was supposed to be training. It was as if he had traveled back in time to when he was young. His hatred of his father and idealization of his grandfather were evident as he spoke.

"Fortunately, my grandfather taught me his ways," Fletcher continued. "For which I will be eternally grateful." Fletcher seemed to snap out of his reverie and resumed his guide-like description of the island and its flora and fauna.

The northern part of the island was rocky and barren. On the southeast side of the island, almost flush to the side of the house, a steep cliff jutted downward. Carved into the side of the cliff were stairs that wound down to a beach below. Rebecca saw no boats on the island the entire time.

Nor did she see any telephone lines or electric lines. She suspected the sloping roof on Fletcher's house was designed to catch rain water and store it. The electricity to the house must be supplied by a separate generator, run either by gasoline or a very powerful battery.

The island was entirely self-sufficient.

Near the end of the week they moved their training to the cliffs behind Fletcher's house, which jutted down to a lagoon below. There they practiced rock climbing and evasive movements on the rocky terrain.

Near the end of a long, hot training session they took turns swinging from a rope into the chilly water below. They had endured an entire week of intense physical and mental strain, and they'd all had a great time. Even Cara.

Rebecca swung out over the lagoon, releasing the rope at the highest arc of her swing, and plummeted down into the icy lagoon. She shot into the water like an inverted spear, kicked once on the lagoon bottom, and shot back up again.

Her head broke water in time to see Lee swinging out over the lagoon. He let go of the rope and came plunging down from the stratosphere directly above her. Two strong leg kicks moved her out of danger as Lee plunged into the water with a giant splash.

Rebecca tread water while waiting for Lee to reappear. The

moments stretched and still Lee remained underwater. Rebecca, growing a little nervous, swam over to where Lee had disappeared to the bottom of the lagoon.

Suddenly, he exploded out of the water right in front of her. He spit a mouthful of water at her and cackled loudly. She splashed him back with a wide grin and swam away. Lee hadn't shaved for several days and his dark stubble of a beard gave him a ruggedly handsome look.

Lee followed her. "I'm actually getting into this, aren't you?"

"Yeah. It's pretty cool."

"Fletcher's not pulling any punches with the training, either, I'll tell you that much. I thought I was in good shape before I came here, but by the end of the day, I'm beat."

"Me, too. It is pretty strenuous. But at least we should be able to keep up with the kids coming over here in a few days."

"Where do you think he's going to keep all these kids? And what are *they* going to eat?" Lee asked.

"What do you mean?"

"I mean, we're six teenagers in peak condition and we have to work full time at staying alive out here. Does Fletcher really think a bunch of little kids will be able to do the same?"

"I guess that's why he's training us. To train them."

"I don't know. I can't see a bunch of little kids living out here in tents and scrounging for their own food."

Rebecca was quiet for a moment as she tread water. "Me, neither." She shrugged. "But that's his problem. As long as he pays us at the end of the summer, right?"

"Right," Lee said, with little conviction.

"And in the meantime, we get a good workout. I think I even lost a few pounds."

A malicious grin came over Lee's face. "Where?" She let out a squeal as he pinched her butt beneath the surface of the water. "There?"

She splashed him and swam away. He swam after her, but with a few strong, sturdy backstrokes she easily put some distance between them. Lee tread water a few yards away with a big happy grin on his face. "I forgot you won all those swim meets."

"Now you know how I got so good."

After their swim they checked their traps and found a young buck caught in a snare, struggling to escape. Until then they had only caught a few rabbits, and the armadillo, although the fishing nets Fletcher had shown them how to set were a great success.

Rebecca felt sorry for the panicked deer, but Fletcher was pleased with the catch. He pulled the large pistol he always carried from his belt and shot the buck behind the ear, killing it instantly.

The boys dragged the deer back to camp and Fletcher demonstrated the proper method for skinning and gutting a large animal. He strung the deer up by its hind legs from a tree limb and placed an empty bucket beneath the head. Then he cut the animal's throat with his hunting knife.

Cara started to retch and rushed behind a bush. Hearing Cara vomiting made Rebecca even more nauseous, but she was determined not to show it. Brian and Kevin looked sick, but Lee was watching with morbid fascination as blood oozed into the bucket.

"We cut the throat to drain the blood," Fletcher explained. "When the blood is drained, boil it thoroughly. It's a valuable source of food and salt."

Rebecca watched as long as she could before looking away.

Skinning rabbits was bad enough, but this was infinitely grosser. She didn't know how much more of this she could take. Fletcher went to work with the knife again. His voice, gruffly mesmerizing, brought her attention back to the deer carcass.

"Make a ring cut at the knee and elbow joints and a Y cut down the front of each of the hind legs and down the belly as far as the throat. Make a cut down each foreleg. Make a clean circular cut around the sex organs . . ."

"Ouch," Kevin said with a wince.

Fletcher continued. ". . . working from the knee downward, remove the skin." Fletcher did so. The skin peeled off like a well-fitted glove. "Then gut the animal." Fletcher cut open the belly and hot guts spilled out steaming into the cool evening air.

Unfortunately for Cara, she chose that moment to rejoin the group. She took one look at the steaming pile and rushed back to the edge of the woods with her hand over her mouth.

Rebecca averted her gaze from the deer carcass, and she noticed the others did the same.

Except for Melanie.

Fletcher continued with the demonstration. "Pin the flesh back with skewers and remove the entrails from the windpipe upward, clearing the entire mass with a firm circular cut. Save the kidneys, liver, and heart, and check these organs for spots or worms. Do not throw away any part of the animal. The glands and entrails and reproductive organs can be used to bait your traps. All parts of the animal are edible, including the meaty parts of the skull such as the eyes, tongue, brain."

Rebecca made a silent vow to become a vegetarian.

"When you've finished butchering the animal, skin it. The skin may be cured by removing all excess flesh and stretching the hide on a frame. The skin of the animal, when dried, is light and good insulation. Or, if one wishes to stuff the animal at a later date, the skin will be well preserved by using this method."

Fletcher seemed pleased when Melanie volunteered to help him skin the deer.

Rebecca hurried across the camp ground to use the little one-person shower while there was still some water left. She looked up into the sky and saw the sun dipping behind a cluster of pine trees. A pale crescent moon was on the rise.

The smell of sizzling meat was wafting through the air. Brian and Kevin were turning the deer over a spit they had built with Fletcher's help. Two forked branches served as poles to hold up a third branch, which had been shoved through the deer from tip to tail. Beneath it a rock-enclosed fire burned heartily.

Rebecca entered the primitive, but effective shower. It consisted of three thin wooden walls and a creaky wooden door fastened by a hook. The water for the shower had to be fetched by hand and poured into a large trough that hung above it, where it was warmed by the sun.

Rebecca yanked on a rusty chain, releasing the water, dousing herself just enough to get wet. She released the chain to save water, then she soaped up and quickly rinsed off. She finished her shower and hurried, shivering, to her tent with a towel tightly wrapped around her.

She had just finished dressing when she heard Cara's angry voice blaring across the camp ground. "All right! Who did it!"

Rebecca poked her head through the tent flap in time to

see Cara come bounding across the campground, wrapped in a towel. Her hair was still full of suds.

"Which one of you idiots used up all the water?" Cara bellowed.

"It was Rebecca," Melanie said. "She used the shower last."

Rebecca slipped out of her tent and joined the others at the campfire. "I thought there was still plenty of water left."

Cara turned and glared at Rebecca. "We don't exactly have plumbing out here, you know!"

"There should be plenty of water in that trough for all of us to take a shower before refilling it," Lee said. "If you'd just lather up and rinse off like you're supposed to."

"I take a long shower," Cara grumbled. "Even if it is cold."

"Then why don't you take a long, cold walk down to the stream and get more water for the shower," Lee suggested.

"Why don't you jump on that stick with the deer and fry yourself, Lee," Melanie said.

"Yeah," Kevin agreed.

"Why don't you go down to the stream with Cara, Melanie," Lee suggested. "And while you're there you can wash out your dirty little mouth."

"Why don't you just shut up, Spinelli?" Kevin said.

"Who asked you anything?" Lee asked.

"Maybe I like Melanie's dirty little mouth," Kevin said. "And maybe I'm getting tired of your bossy attitude all the time when Fletcher's not around. I get enough of that back at the Academy."

"You'd better get used to it . . ."

Kevin made a move toward Lee, but Brian held him back. He shoved a monogrammed flask into the big guy's meaty

THE KILLING GAME

hand. Kevin took a long hit, and a glazed look passed over his ruddy face as the liquor hit home. He went back to turning the deer on the spit, but he still glared at Lee.

"Hey, Cara, I've got something right here to warm you up." Brian held out a monogrammed flask to her. He and Kevin had been drinking heavily every night.

Cara hesitated, then took the flask. "Why not?" She took a drink and made a face as the warm liquor burned the back of her throat, but she managed to hold it down. She passed the flask back to Brian, who took a drink and offered it to Melanie.

Melanie also took a big gulp. She swayed a little, walked up to Lee, and held out the flask. "C'mon, let's be friends," she said in a suggestive voice.

Lee just shook his head.

Melanie shrugged, took another gulp from the flask, and braced herself as the booze did its thing. Then she walked over to Kevin, who had been watching her intently the entire time, and held out the flask to him. He took the flask, and Melanie's hand, and pulled her to him.

Melanie didn't seem to object. She just stared coldly at Lee as Kevin held her close to him with one hand, and drank from the flask with the other.

The meat sizzled on the spit.

"Don't let it burn, sport," Brian said to Kevin.

"Maybe I can help," Melanie said, giving the deer a twirl as Kevin still held on to her.

Cara looked at Brian. "Isn't this turning into a cozy little love nest?"

"And no parents to bug us." Brian smiled wickedly. "C'mon, there's still some water in the drinking bucket. I'll help you finish your shower."

Cara kept her eyes locked with his. "And then what?"

"Then I guess we'll have to go down to the stream for more."

"My knight in shining armor," Cara said sarcastically.

Brian nodded toward Melanie who was snuggling up to Kevin, then turned back to Cara. "Like the girl said, let's be friends."

Cara chuckled. Then she whirled around and headed back to the shower, followed by Brian, who paused only long enough to fetch the bucket of drinking water before hurrying after her.

"I guess they're back together," Rebecca said to Lee in a soft voice.

"Well, you know what they say. Birds of a feather flock together."

Rebecca slapped her forearm, killing a mosquito and leaving a bloody smear. Swarms of bugs had plagued Rebecca since they arrived and she reached beneath her sweater and scratched one of the many tiny red bumps dotting her skin.

No one else was getting bit, although Cara had a bad sunburn across her back from when she had fallen asleep lying in the sun one afternoon.

Rebecca shooed away another buzzing mosquito.

"It must be your deodorant attracting them," Lee said as he sidled up next to her.

"I'm not wearing any."

He nuzzled her ear. "You mean you always smell this good?"

She leaned back into him. "Uh-huh."

"I have something I can rub on your bites," Lee suggested.

Rebecca smiled and looked up at him. "I bet you do." She swatted another mosquito.

Melanie and Kevin were now sitting on the big log near

THE KILLING GAME

the campfire. Rebecca could see them through the licking tongues of flame; they were engaged in some heavy necking. Then, even as Kevin continued to kiss her, Melanie turned and stared at her.

A cool breeze swept over the camp, making the camp fire flicker.

Rebecca turned away from Melanie's probing eyes "Let's go into my tent," she whispered. She could feel Lee's heart beating right through his sweatshirt, almost as hard as her own.

"Okay." His voice was raspy with anticipation.

When they got inside the tent, Lee pulled a small spray can of antiseptic from his back pocket. "C'mon," he said. "Pull up your sweater."

Rebecca chuckled and turned her back to him. She pulled up her sweater; she wasn't wearing a bra. She had been flirting heavily with Lee for days now, wondering all along just how far she should let it go.

She glanced out the little flap window of her tent and could see Kevin and Melanie, now standing, tending to the deer. Kevin was saying something to Melanie, who only half-listened, as she turned to face Rebecca's tent.

Rebecca was distracted from Melanie's gaze when Lee sprayed her back with the antiseptic. It felt cool and stopped the itching right away. Then he dropped the spray can to the tent floor and kneaded the tense muscles of her back with his large strong hands.

She felt the front of her sweater creeping up toward her breasts but made no effort to pull it down. Lee's touch felt so nice.

Then, Lee's hands began to stray where there were no bug bites. And that's when she saw it.

Creeping out of her sleeping bag.

The snake reared its ugly diamond-shaped head and looked

at them for an agonizingly long moment, its forked tongue flicking between two needle sharp fangs.

Then, it began to slither toward them.

Twelve

"Lee!" Rebecca screamed "Look!"

Lee whirled and saw the snake. He quickly picked up the can of antiseptic spray from the tent floor and sprayed it into the snake's eyes.

The snake made a stabbing motion at Lee with its fangs before rapidly retreating to other side of the tent, where it coiled up by the tent door and stared menacingly at the two of them.

Rebecca's pulse quickened. "It's just waiting for us by the door. We can't get past it."

"I guess we'll have to go out the back door, then." Lee kept his eyes on the snake as he removed the switchblade from his back pocket. He flicked it open and jabbed the point of the blade into the tent wall. He yanked up, tearing a large gash into the fabric.

The snake was on the move again. It disappeared beneath a mound of dirty clothes.

"Hurry up." Lee motioned to the tear in the tent and Rebecca slipped through it. Lee quickly followed.

Now, safely outside the tent and away from the menacing snake, Lee's cool manner abruptly disappeared. "Someone put that damn snake in your tent and I think I know who."

Rebecca followed Lee as he strode across the campground to where Melanie and Kevin sat on the log by the campfire, eating deer meat with their bare hands. The meat was still a little rare, and blood was dripping down their hands. Melanie looked up with a malicious grin as they approached.

"Did you put that snake in Rebecca's tent?" Lee asked her, the anger rising in his voice.

"Was it poisonous?" she asked nonchalantly.

Lee glared at her angrily. "What am I, some snake expert or something? It was a snake. It had fangs, the tongue, the whole bit. Did you put that in there or what?"

Kevin rose to his feet and tossed a deer bone into the fire. He looked at Lee. "Just because it was in Rebecca's tent doesn't mean one of us *put* it in there. It could've gotten in on its own."

"I keep the door flap zipped up at all times," Rebecca said. "To keep the bugs out. Like I've done every day since we've been here."

"Where was it when you found it?" Kevin asked.

"It was hiding in my sleeping bag," Rebecca said.

"One of the first things Fletcher told us was to shake out our stuff for snakes," Kevin said, rubbing his hand over his scrub brush haircut. "You should've checked the sleeping bag."

"I know Rebecca. She did check it earlier. She's very thorough. That's why I think someone *put* the snake in her tent," Lee said. "Her!" He was pointing to Melanie.

"Yeah? Well, maybe *I* did it," Kevin said.

"Yeah? Well, then maybe you should go in there and get it out," Lee said.

It was a direct challenge, Rebecca knew, and Kevin was clearly debating whether or not to take Lee up on it. It would have been a good fight. Although Kevin was at least a head taller than Lee and probably had fifty pounds on him, he lacked Lee's carved musculature, his quick reflexes.

Kevin ripped off another piece of deer meat from the smoking carcass. The fire had died down somewhat. "I said *maybe* I did." Without Brian around to hold him back Kevin didn't seem quite as brave.

"Look, guys," Rebecca said. "I'm not going to make a big deal of this, but I just want to remind you that Mr. Fletcher has tried to teach us that we have to work as a *team* in order to survive in the wilderness. Well, my idea of teamwork and bonding isn't throwing a snake inside someone's tent—"

"Bonding?" Melanie snorted. "Your idea of *bonding* is to sneak off by yourselves and fool around."

Lee stepped between Melanie and Rebecca. "Knock it off, you two!" Then he turned and faced Kevin and Melanie. "I catch anyone sticking a snake in Rebecca's tent or committing any other act of sabotage, they're going to have to answer to me. That snake could've been poisonous. Someone could've gotten killed."

"Are you threatening me, Lee Spinelli?" Melanie asked, walking boldly toward him.

"I'm *warning* you," Lee said, taking Rebecca by the arm and leading her away.

"I don't like to be threatened," Rebecca could hear Melanie saying in a low and menacing voice as she and Lee walked away from the campfire, back toward her tent.

Rebecca took a deep breath to calm down. "So . . . how are we supposed to get rid of it?"

"You mean Melanie or the snake?"

Rebecca chuckled. "Can we get rid of that snake in my tent, first?"

"Yeah, I guess," Lee said distractedly as he looked back at the campfire.

"Lee? Why would Melanie put a snake in my tent?"

"Why else? To get back at me."

"But why?"

Lee frowned darkly. "It's a long story."

Rebecca gave him her most winning smile "Well, I'm not doing anything the rest of the night. Want to tell it to me?"

Lee grinned weakly. "Yeah. Maybe. But let's get rid of that snake first." They walked around to the back of the tent in time to see the snake slithering through the gash left by Lee's switchblade.

Rebecca halted in her tracks at the sight of the gruesome reptile, her blood turning cold. "Ugh."

"I just hope that was the only one in there." Lee kicked some dirt in its direction to hurry it along. When the snake had safely vanished into the thick undergrowth, Lee slipped back inside the tent.

"See any more snakes in there?" Rebecca asked.

"No," came Lee's voice from inside the tent. "But you have some other visitors in here."

Rebecca cautiously peeked inside the tent. She didn't see any more snakes, but there were approximately two million bugs clustered around her Coleman Lantern, which still burned brightly. "Oh, no," she moaned.

Lee was already opening the flap doors and trying to shoo some of the bugs out.

"How am I ever going to get rid of these bugs?" she asked. Even as she asked it a few more flew back inside the tent.

"Take the lantern out and most of them will probably follow. And we can light up some mosquito coils, too. That might help."

She inspected the tear in the tent wall, about four feet in length. "Then how do I keep them from coming back in?"

Lee eyed the gash in the tent. Then, he looked at Rebecca with a mischievous grin. "Well . . . we can always share my tent."

Rebecca couldn't tell if he was joking or not. Then he pulled her to him and kissed her hard. She kissed him back, just as hard.

THE KILLING GAME

Lee broke the kiss as an extremely large mosquito landed on the tip of his nose. He flicked the bug away. It disappeared back through the gash in the tent. "Unfortunately, the one thing I didn't bring on this trip was needle and thread. I'll bet Fletcher has some, though. Why don't you check with him while I try to get rid of these bugs."

Rebecca nodded. She gave him another little kiss before stepping through the tent flaps and jogging up the hill toward Fletcher's house.

It grew dark on her way up the hill. She regretted not bringing a flashlight.

She looked up the sloping hill to where Fletcher's house stood, like a white and gleaming fortress guarding the island. The back of the house was framed by woods of fragrant, tall, blue-green pines. Behind the trees, the rocky, craggy cliffs stood as silent sentries to the sea.

She thought she heard a twig snap in the woods off to the side, in front of her.

She stopped and listened.

A rustling.

It stopped.

She remembered a book she had once read on the history of New England. It was rumored that many of the old houses and inns and hotels that had stood since colonial days were still possessed by ghosts. She thought about what Jenny had said about the island, and felt her body go tense. If ghosts did exist at all, they would certainly be on this spooky island, she reasoned.

The wind whipped up with a fury, bending the treetops to its will.

She heard another twig snap.

Behind her, this time. From a clump of bushes. Her eyes scanned the woods, expecting something to suddenly come bounding at her, but all was quiet again. She looked back up at Fletcher's house. For a brief moment, it seemed as if it were a giant wolf head peering down at her from above.

The bushes behind her parted and something came darting out of them, sending her heart shooting into her throat.

Only a raccoon.

She watched the animal disappear into the woods across the trail. She could've sworn it was grinning at her as it ran past. Could animals grin? She emitted a nervous little laugh. They seemed to in these woods.

Even the animals they caught in their snares seemed to be grinning at them as they faced their doom. As if to say 'Oh, sure, we're caught in the trap, but so are you . . . so are you . . . you just don't know it.'

She could hear the animal moving through the bushes, heading up the hill, almost parallel to her.

Near the top of the hill she cast one last glance into the woods, thinking to see her furry escort, and saw an eye gleaming in the darkness.

Just one eye.

Staring at her.

She stared back at the eye, her heart pounding.

The eye disappeared.

Briefly, outlined in the moonlit sky, she saw a tall, angular man running across the clearing between the edge of the woods and the house.

"Mr. Fletcher?" she called, although she knew it couldn't be Fletcher—he wasn't tall or angular. Did Mr. Fletcher have an assistant they didn't know about?

They hadn't seen one, and he hadn't mentioned any.

She stood frozen on the path. Then she saw the man again as he approached Fletcher's front door. Suddenly, the door opened with a flash of light and closed again as the man slipped inside the house.

Haltingly, Rebecca made her way up the rest of the hill

THE KILLING GAME

and across the cobbled walk that led to Fletcher's front door. She turned the doorknob but the door was locked.

She knocked on the door.

No answer.

She banged on the door.

Still no answer.

She banged harder—and she felt something warm against the cool skin of her breasts. She placed her hand to her chest. It was the pendant. She removed the thin chain with the skull key from her neck and stared at it. The skull was glowing gently in the pale light of the luminous moon.

Skull key.

Skull.

Skeleton.

Skeleton key.

Skeleton key.

It's a skeleton key. With a trembling hand she slowly inserted the key into the lock of the heavy wooden front door and turned it part way. The lock resisted, so she reversed the motion. Still no give. Frustrated, she twisted it sharply.

The lock gave with an audible click.

She pushed the door open and it moved away from her as if it had a mind of its own. She slipped the pendant over her head again. Ignoring the knot twisting inside her stomach, she stepped inside the house.

It was almost pitch black in the banquet hall, except for the moonlight that crept in through the opened door. Rebecca felt along the wall for a light switch but found none. She stopped for a moment to give her eyes time to adjust to the darkness.

A radio transmitter crackled from somewhere inside the house.

She stood perfectly still, listening There it was again. It

came from the end of a long hallway at the opposite end of the banquet hall.

Slowly she made her way across the banquet hall floor, wincing at every squeak her sneakers made as they pressed against the smooth stone floor. The squeaks seemed to echo through the entire house, bouncing off every wall.

The front door slammed shut with a bang.

Rebecca jumped at the sudden sound. She whirled around, took a step backward, and fell over something stretched across banquet hall floor.

Something hard and hairy.

Like a human head.

She froze, petrified with fear. Her heart was beating so hard she feared it might knock a hole in her chest. She peered into the darkness, straining to see what it was she had fallen over. Slowly, the dark hairy form on the banquet hall floor took on a more specific shape.

The bear rug.

Then something whispered her name.

Rebeccaaaaa . . .

This is getting really weird, Rebecca thought.

Rebeccaaaaa . . .

She wanted to roll up in a fetal position and wait for this bad dream to go away. She felt incredibly vulnerable in the strange, dark house.

She listened again for her whispered name. She was answered with a gentle breeze, blowing through the expansive room.

Maybe it was just the wind, she thought, her nerves drawn tight, refusing to admit that she shared the room with a ghost. She tried to convince herself that she had only imagined she heard her name whispered. She took a deep breath and stood up. She was tired of playing games in the dark. "Mr. Fletcher!"

Her voice echoed back to her.

"Mr. Fletcher!" she bellowed.

The radio crackled again in the darkness.

She crossed to the entrance of the hallway and peered down it. The hallway was lit by a glimmer of dim lights that ran along the floor molding.

The crackle of the short wave radio was much louder in the enclosed hallway. It came from behind a door at the end of the hallway.

She made her way down the creaking hallway to the door and raised her hand to knock on it. She stopped when she heard voices from behind the door. She put her ear to it and listened.

"I told you to stay out of sight, Jorge," the voice was saying. Fletcher's voice. "I don't want you running around the island at night, arousing suspicion."

"But Eduardo," an accented voice answered him. "It is so stuffy in that little shack. I can not breathe."

"Why don't you just open the damn door?"

"Then it is too cold. The ocean breeze chills my bones."

"You're just a whiner. A nosy whiner. Do you think I don't know that you're spying on those kids?"

"How much longer must we stay here? You told me you hated this island."

"I do, you little fool. Why do you think I'm selling it?"

"When are the others coming?"

"Soon now. Be patient. I'm trying to raise them on the radio. Now stop your crying and return to your hole in the rock until I come for you." The words were harsh, but the tone was affectionate.

There was a pause, then Rebecca jumped as the doorknob suddenly turned. She turned and raced back down the hallway as Fletcher's door opened and filled the corridor with light.

She ducked into an adjoining hallway and leaned close to the wall.

Footsteps padded her way. A tall, thin man walked past her. She leaned closer to the wall. The footsteps receded into the darkness and silence.

Her head bumped something. She leaned back and saw an object glinting in the light. She stepped back and noticed, hanging from the wall, a row of framed pictures, the muted hallway light reflecting off the glass that enclosed them. In fact, the entire hallway wall was covered with them.

She studied the one closest to her. It was an old, grainy black and white photograph. An elderly man with a head of unkempt snowy white hair stood proudly next to a fallen lion, the butt of a long hunting rifle resting upon its head.

Standing next to the proud hunter was another man, middle-aged but with longish gray hair, who looked out of the picture with a thousand mile stare. He didn't seem too happy to be there.

Kneeling next to the lion with a broad smile on his face, looking up in admiration at the great white-haired hunter, was a little boy. Despite the grainy quality of the picture, and the muted light of the hallway, Rebecca easily recognized the little boy.

He was Edward Fletcher.

The lion killer must be his grandfather.

The unhappy man, his father.

At the end of the hallway stood another door. Rebecca walked down the hall to it and twisted the doorknob. Also locked. She slipped the skeleton key from around her neck and placed it into the keyhole. She gave it a turn. The door unlocked. She pushed open the door.

Moonlight filtered into the small room from a tiny window high up on one wall. Every square inch of the rest of the walls were covered with weapons of every description: Maces, knives, daggers, swords, bows and arrows. One wall held nothing but a large, locked weapons rack filled with hunting rifles.

She heard the crackle of radio static again.

She left the weapons room, silently pulling the door shut behind her, and walked back down the small hallway to the main corridor. The radio was crackling louder, now. On tiptoes she crept down to Fletcher's door.

The walls, for an agonizingly long moment, felt as if they were closing in upon her.

She fought off the claustrophobic feeling and put her ear to the door. "Is it time to begin The Killing Game?" she heard a voice through the radio cough.

"Yes," barked Fletcher's voice. "As soon as you arrive, The Killing Game will begin."

Thirteen

Rebecca stood outside the door, her body rigid.
The Killing Game.
She wondered what he meant by that.
Rebeccaaaaa . . .
The hairs on the back of her neck stood straight up. She turned and stared down the dark hallway. And saw nothing. Rebecca walked slowly back down the hallway. She felt the sweat on her forehead turning colder with every step she took. This must be what it's like to be insane, she thought. Rebecca didn't believe in ghosts, but then she had never heard one call her name before.
Rebeccaaaaa!
The ghostly whisper was coming from behind the door to the weapons room, now cracked slightly open. Propelled by a sudden surge of panic Rebecca ran straight ahead down the length of the main hallway and into the banquet hall.

She ran as fast as she could, breaking stride only once to hurdle the big bear rug, and didn't stop until she reached the front door, which she threw open with a bang.

She was staring at the cold night, at freedom.

She didn't stop running until she was safely back in camp. Lee looked up when he saw her coming toward him. He held the edge of a large mosquito net in his hand; the rest of it was draped over her tent. He dropped the net as she ran into his arms.

"What's wrong? What happened?" Lee asked.

Gulping air, Rebecca struggled to stop the heaving of her chest. "A ghost! It called out my name!"

There was a pause before Lee broke out into a spasm of giggles. Rebecca glared at him.

"A ghost?" he asked, shaking his head from side to side. His giggling turned to convulsive laughter as he looked up the hill at the gleaming white house. "I knew I shouldn't have let you go up there alone!"

Rebecca's anger turned to embarrassment. "Okay, I don't know if there was a *ghost* up there or not but there was definitely *somebody* up there."

"Yeah," Lee said. "His name is Fletcher. He *lives* up there." He broke out into laughter again.

Rebecca's embarrassment turned to anger again. Enough was enough. She pushed Lee hard against his chest. He wasn't expecting it and toppled backwards. "Not *Fletcher!* There was someone else up there!"

Lee looked up from where he had fallen with a slightly more sober attitude. Rebecca immediately regretted pushing him but had no intention of apologizing. Fortunately, Lee didn't seem to hold a grudge.

"Well, Brian and Cara went down the hill to fetch a pail of water," he said. "And then Melanie just flat took off."

Rebecca watched Kevin turning the deer on the spit, his vacant stare fueling the flickering fire. She always found it hard to read Kevin's expression. But maybe that was because that mask of stupidity he wore wasn't a mask at all. Maybe he really had no thoughts in his head.

Lee stood up and dusted himself off. "Ever since Melanie unhooked herself from him, Kevin's been here playing with the spit. That much I can vouch for," Lee said. "But as for the other three—"

"There was another man, Lee," Rebecca interrupted. "A

stranger. I saw him in the house. A tall, skinny man. I think his name is Jorge."

"Jorge?"

"Yeah."

Lee gave it some thought. "Are you sure?"

"Positive."

Lee was quiet for a moment as he looked up the hill at the gleaming white house. Then he strode to his tent and unzipped the front flap, reached in and pulled out his black leather jacket. He slipped it on, rezipped the tent flap, turned and faced Rebecca. "Let's go," was all he said.

"Where?" Rebecca asked. But she knew where. Back up the hill to that spooky house.

"Let's go see who's up there besides Fletcher." His tone was grim, determined. "Because I don't believe in ghosts."

He was calling her bluff, Rebecca knew, so she made up her mind to play out her hand. She went to her tent and got her hunting knife and slipped it into the waistband of her jeans. Then she grabbed two flashlights and gave one to Lee.

Lee snapped his flashlight on, then off, to check the power. Rebecca did the same. "Don't use it unless you have to," he warned. "Follow me. Move fast and stay low."

She nodded. Lee took off at a jog and she followed close at his heels. About a third of the way up the hill, Lee slowed to a stop. "Let's get off the main path."

They took a narrower path that curved through thick woods of pines and birch trees, still deep with brown, dead winter leaves. Lee occasionally flicked on the flashlight to help them keep their bearings.

They entered a small clearing and Rebecca saw Lee ahead of her, outlined by the moon. Rebecca's heartbeat accelerated. Hormones had finally caught up to her. She realized she had an almost overwhelming desire to make out with Lee Spinelli.

Right here, right now, right in the woods.

Lee quickly crossed the clearing, moving with the easy grace of a natural athlete. In his black leather jacket he reminded her of a sleek panther. She hurried to catch him. They passed into the woods again. Fresh, sweet smelling woods.

She grabbed Lee by the arm, momentarily startling him, and pulled him behind a large birch tree. She wasn't exactly sure how a girl was supposed to seduce a boy, especially in these primitive conditions. She leaned in close and felt Lee's body suddenly go tight.

"Yeah, I see him, too," Lee said in a harsh whisper.

"See who—"

"Shhh."

Then she saw him. Moving stealthily down the narrow path toward them. The tall, angular man walked past them and continued down the path.

"I think that was him," Rebecca whispered.

"Who?"

"The guy I saw earlier tonight."

They stayed snuggled against the tree until the stranger's footsteps had completely receded into the gloom of the woods.

"Let's follow him," Lee said.

Rebecca squeezed his hand in reply and they hurried after the tall skinny man. They watched him cross the main path and take another path they knew led down to the stream where they filled their water buckets. Near the stream the man stopped and crouched behind an uprooted tree stump.

They crept up behind him.

Through a gap in the trees Rebecca could see all the way to the stream. Intertwined on a large blanket near the bank, with their clothes a rumpled mess about them, were Cara and Brian.

They were making love!

Rebecca gasped loudly.

The skinny guy spun around. Lee shown the flashlight directly on his swarthy, pockmarked face. He appeared to be in his early twenties, and looked like some kind of Indian, with his high cheekbones and jet black hair.

And he had a patch over one eye.

The man bolted through the bushes. Cara and Brian bellowed in surprise as he hurdled them and splashed into the stream. Lee shot off after him, but he didn't get far. His foot became entangled with a large, gnarly root and he plummeted to the ground.

Lee rolled almost all the way to the stream bank before coming to a stop. He grabbed his ankle in pain as Rebecca ran to his aid. "Are you all right?" she asked, as Lee sat up rubbing his ankle.

"I think so," he muttered in disgust, rising gingerly to his feet.

"Who the hell was that?" Cara demanded in a high, shrill voice as she tugged on her clothes. Her red hair was bobbing about like an erupted volcano.

"I don't know." Lee took a few delicate steps to test his tender ankle.

"Should we report him to Fletcher?" Cara asked, buttoning up her Levis.

"I think he *works* for Fletcher," Rebecca said. "I heard Fletcher call him Jorge."

Brian stood before them in his Hudson Military Academy letter jacket and boxer shorts, a befuddled look on his face. He still appeared to be a bit drunk. "What the hell is going on?"

"Who is Jorge?" Cara demanded.

"I . . . I overheard Mr. Fletcher talking to someone in his

room. He called him Jorge. And I also overheard him talking to someone on a short-wave radio."

"You've had a busy little night, haven't you?" Cara asked, a bit nastily. "Who else have you been spying on?"

"I wasn't spying. I went up to the house to see Fletcher about getting something to repair my tent and I heard . . . I heard him say . . . say something about . . ."

"About what?" Cara asked impatiently.

"A *Killing Game.*"

There was a long quiet moment before Brian finally broke the silence. "Killing Game? What the hell is that supposed to mean?"

Lee was giving her a funny look. "Was this before or after the ghost called your name?"

"What ghost?" Brian asked, a little nervously. "Are you saying that man with the patch on his eye was a ghost!"

"He's probably some guy Fletcher's got spying on us," Cara said. "I wouldn't put it past that old pervert."

"At least this proves one thing," Rebecca said. "I wasn't imagining things the first night on the island when I said I saw someone in the woods spying on us. Someone with one eye—"

"Jorge," Lee said. "With the patch over his eye."

"You mean every time Brian and I have come down to the stream together this guy's been spying on us?" Cara asked, the color draining from her face.

"Could be," Lee said with a smirk. "You missed a button, by the way," he said, pointing to the crotch of her jeans.

Cara finished buttoning up before sashaying over to where the blanket lay. She whipped it off the ground, shook twigs and dead leaves from it, and folded it up into a tight little square.

"This island is really starting to make me sick!" Cara suddenly shouted. "You can't . . . can't even . . . *get water* without someone spying on you!"

An owl hooted in response.

"What do you think he meant by *The Killing Game?*" Lee asked Rebecca.

"I don't know. It was just something I overheard," Rebecca said. She wasn't sure she wanted to know what Fletcher meant.

Lee flicked on his flashlight, which he had managed to hold onto during his somersault routine, then flicked it off again. It was in no worse shape than the rest of his body. "Ready?"

"For what?"

"For anything."

Rebecca smiled. "If you are."

Lee smiled back. Without another word, they silently made their way back the way they had come, leaving Brian and Cara to return to the camp.

The path led them to a clearing not far from the northwest wall of the house. Lee walked to the middle of the clearing, knelt down, and smelt the grass. "I figured as much."

"What?" Rebecca asked.

"Gas."

"Gas?"

"This is an airfield."

"It isn't big enough to be an airfield."

"It's big enough to land a helicopter." Lee looked over at the house. "What else did you find in the house?"

"A bunch of photographs of Fletcher's father and grandfather, a room full of weapons—"

"A room full of weapons?"

"Yeah."

"What kind of weapons?"

"All sorts. Sword and knives and guns and stuff."

THE KILLING GAME

"What kind of guns?"

Rebecca shrugged. "Rifles and stuff. I don't really know too much about guns."

"I do," Lee said confidently. "My dad's a collector. I'd like to see some of those guns."

"I could show them to you," Rebecca said.

Lee looked puzzled. "I'm surprised he doesn't keep that stuff locked up."

"He does," Rebecca said. Now Lee looked more puzzled than ever. "I unlocked the door."

"How?"

"With the key Jenny Demos gave me. It's a skeleton key."

Lee stared at her with a befuddled look on his face. "I'm waiting for the punch line to the joke."

"There is no joke. This key can open any lock."

"You're kidding?"

"I can prove it to you," Rebecca said with a smug smile.

"Okay, let's go," Lee said, skepticism tinging his voice.

The front door was still unlocked, which reminded Rebecca that she had also left the weapons room unlocked. She had meant to relock them both before she had bolted like a frightened colt.

They entered the house—it was darker inside than outside—and paused long enough for their eyes to adjust to the gloom.

Rebecca pointed to the opposite end of the banquet hall. "Fletcher's room is at the end of that hallway. That's where I heard the radio crackle."

Lee nodded and started to make his way across the cold stone floor of the banquet hall.

"Watch out for the bear rug," Rebecca cautioned, momentarily flicking on her flashlight to show Lee where the rug sat.

The bear head stared back at them with that stony silence that death brings to all things.

Rebecca's heart thudded into her chest. "Oh!" she gasped. Lee pulled her close to him. "What?"

"When I flicked on the light . . . I saw someone in the shadows."

"Where?" Lee rasped.

She pointed back toward the banquet table. Lee aimed his flashlight at the table and flicked the light on. The yellow beam failed to reveal anything in its cone of light.

Lee shone his light around the room. About thirty feet behind the long wooden table, in another corner of the banquet hall, stood a door, swinging slightly.

"I think whoever it was took off through the kitchen door," Lee said in a soft voice. He continued to watch the door until the swinging stopped altogether. "C'mon, show me that room with the guns."

They crept across the banquet hall and entered the corridor that led to Fletcher's room. They tiptoed down the long hallway toward the crack of light that bled from beneath his door.

Rebecca could no longer hear the radio crackling. She stopped at the entrance to the smaller, adjoining hallway—the photo gallery hallway. "It's down there," she said, motioning to the end of the hallway.

"The room with the guns?"

"Yeah. And the hallway of pictures."

Then they heard something coming from the end of the main corridor. From Fletcher's room.

And it wasn't a crackling radio.

They stood transfixed in the darkness, staring mutely at the door.

They heard it again.

A high squeaky sound, as if something were in pain.

"What the hell is that?" Lee asked. He stealthily made his way down the hall to Fletcher's door, followed closely by

Rebecca. Lee put his ear to the door. Then he smirked and chuckled softly.

"What?" Rebecca whispered.

Lee motioned to the door. Rebecca put her ear to it. Strange, soft music floated to her ear.

"Fletcher's playing the violin," Lee whispered. "Or trying to."

Rebecca grinned as tension seeped out of her body. Then she felt Lee tugging at her sleeve. She nodded and followed Lee back down the small corridor that led to the weapons room. Rebecca pointed out the photo of the three generations of Fletchers.

Lee studied the picture with intense interest. "Fletcher's old man looks like an aging hippie," Lee said.

Unlike the grandfather, Rebecca thought, who looked more like a villain from a Tarzan movie, one of the elephant poachers who kills for ivory until the claws of a lion or Tarzan's avenging hands end his scummy life.

Lee shone his flashlight along the wall to reveal photographs of hunters on safari, kneeling beside or standing proudly next to dead animals. Their trophies, game of every description, from birds to lions.

It was the last picture on the wall that really rattled Rebecca.

It was an old, crinkled snapshot—it looked as if someone had carried it in his pocket for a long length of time—of a rather fierce looking warrior. A dark face, with white stripes painted across each wrinkled, sunken cheek, glared at the camera. A headdress of jungle bird feathers covered his head, and a tiny bone pierced his nostrils. Lips were drawn back to display black, jagged teeth.

It was enough to give you the creeps.

Behind him stood a line of younger, less important-looking, spear wielding warriors.

But standing right next to the important warrior, with his arm draped across the man's sagging shoulders, was Edward Fletcher.

Fourteen

"Jesus," Lee said, inspecting the picture. "These guys look like cannibals or something."

"I think they're Brazilian Indians," Rebecca said, recalling a *National Geographic* special she recently had seen on TV in the rec room at the riding academy. "From the Amazon or someplace."

"Weird," Lee said, shaking his head. "And Fletcher seems to be pals with them. What do you think, Rebecca? Is ol' Fletcher a cannibal?"

Rebecca laughed uneasily. "I don't know, but Jorge might be. He sure looks the part. I'll bet he comes from the same place this picture was taken. One thing's for sure," she said, as she took in the photographs featuring Edward Fletcher with his jungle boot leaving a muddy footprint on the head of some poor dead animal, "he's no animal lover like his father."

Lee was down on his hands and knees examining the floor molding.

"What are you looking for?" Rebecca asked.

"Looking for a place to rig a trip wire. If we have any unwanted visitors, I want to know about it."

Lee found what he was looking for and ran a length of wire across the width of the corridor before fastening it to a loose nail jutting out of an ancient wooden beam. Then he stood up and proudly inspected his handiwork. "A little trick I learned in that book Jenny Demos gave me."

Finding the door still unlocked, Rebecca and Lee entered the weapons room. Lee closed the door behind them and ran a beam of light over each wall. "I was afraid of that," Lee grumbled.

"What?"

His light played on a vacant spot on the wall, the only vacant spot in a row of archery weapons. "I'll bet she took one."

Then his light fell upon the rifle rack. With a gleam of admiration in his eye, Lee walked over to examine the well polished wooden stocks of the hunting rifles.

"They've been cleaned recently," Lee said. "I can still smell the gun oil. Which means they were probably used recently. Which means these weapons are no ornaments."

Lee pointed out the rifles to Rebecca, from top to bottom. "Remington 870 Wingmaster, Fox Sterlingworth, Winchester 97, Parker Trojan, Remington 58 Sportsman, Browning 'Sweet Sixteen.' "

"And this baby," he said, running his hands, almost reverentially, over the biggest and baddest looking rifle in the rack, "this is a Weatherby Magnum. You won't find this in your local gun shop. There isn't an animal alive that this thing couldn't knock off its feet. The kick from this thing would definitely knock *you* off your feet, too."

Lee swept his hand over the rack. "These are all high-gauge shotguns. Some of the finest hunting weaponry I've ever seen—" They heard a thud, followed by a muffled curse, coming from the hallway.

Lee flicked off the flashlight.

"I think we've got a visitor," he whispered. They walked cautiously to the door and put their ears to it. They heard muffled footsteps running down the hall. Lee flung open the door but they saw nothing in the dim light.

"Did you see who it was?" Rebecca asked.

"No. But I have a pretty good idea." A dark frown swept across his face. Then he whipped out his switchblade and flicked it open with a menacing click, knelt down, and cut his trip wire. "C'mon, maybe we can still catch her."

They hurried down the main corridor that spilled into the banquet hall. They heard the violin music again, louder than ever now, echoing off the cold stone walls of the deserted hunting lodge.

They had no sooner slipped through the front door when Rebecca heard something whistling through the air. Then an arrow struck the thick wooden door a few inches above and to the right of her head.

Rebecca dove to the ground and pulled Lee with her. Their eyes made contact and Lee pointed to a clump of bushes just off the trail. Rebecca nodded and readied herself. They sprung to their feet, dashed to the bushes, and dove over them.

Another arrow thudded into the tree above them.

"She was crazy," Lee muttered.

"Who, Melanie?"

"Yeah. I told you she was a champion archer. She must've taken a bow and quiver of arrows from that room."

"You mean she wants to *kill* us?" Rebecca asked in disbelief.

"It sure looks that way."

Rebecca noticed a vein on Lee's forehead starting to throb.

"I don't feel like hanging around here all night, waiting to be killed," he said. "She can hit a dime at forty paces and give you nine cents change. I've seen her do it."

Rebecca peeked over the bush and down the long, dark trail. It looked like an endless black tunnel. Somewhere down there, Melanie was waiting for them with a bow in her hand and murder in her heart.

"I wouldn't keep your head exposed for too long," Lee warned. "Or you might be wearing an arrow for a hat."

Rebecca ducked. "What are we going to do?"

Lee shrugged. "What *can* we do? I told you she's nuts."

"We can turn her over to Fletcher."

"I think he's nuttier than she is."

"Are you sure it's her? What if it's Jorge?"

Lee shrugged. He started to crawl away from the bush, commando style. "C'mon, let's go," he said, when he realized Rebecca wasn't following him.

She crawled up alongside him. "Where?"

"Back to camp. We'll take the back trails; it'll be safer that way. Once we're there she won't do anything. Not in front of witnesses."

"Are you sure?"

"No."

About fifteen minutes later, they slipped into camp.

The night sky was clear under a bright moon. Brian and Cara sat before the crackling campfire, eating deer meat. Kevin dozed drunkenly against a log.

Shadows played over their faces as flames from the fire darted and flickered. A boom box was blasting out a Beastie Boys number, "Check Your Head."

"Have either of you seen Melanie?" Lee asked.

The music thumped away. "What?" Brian asked. He washed the deer meat down with a gulp of whiskey from his flask.

Lee reached down and snapped off the cassette player. Brian looked up at Lee. "Well, cuz, what's the problem this time? Is Igor or Jorge or whatever-his-name-is on the loose

THE KILLING GAME 131

again? We really must talk to Fletcher about this. We shouldn't be snooped upon—"

"Have either of you seen Melanie?" Lee asked again in a quiet, intense voice.

"She was in her tent the last time we saw her," Cara said in a tone of voice that was also a dismissal. She turned the tape player back on and went back to chewing on her meat.

The deer meat was still pretty rare, Rebecca couldn't help but notice, as pink juices dribbled down Cara's chin. They all ate with their fingers now, even their cereal in the morning. They were becoming like animals in the wild, Rebecca thought.

Lee looked over in the direction of Melanie's tent. The back of the tent faced the campfire, unlike the other tents. Even in this, Melanie seemed determined to prove her independence.

Lee marched over to Melanie's tent entrance, unzipped the flap, threw it open, and stepped inside.

All hell broke loose.

First, they heard Melanie scream; then, there was a lot of thrashing around, then Melanie screamed again. Finally, she came stumbling out, followed by Lee.

"I told you that guy was an animal," Cara said to Rebecca, looking up from her bloody meal.

Melanie stampeded over to the campfire in T-shirt and panties, her hair disheveled, her face red. She made a bee line to where Kevin still slept, slumped against the log.

"Did you see what he tried to do?" Melanie asked the sleeping Kevin. Getting no response, she looked at Brian and Cara, her eyes wide with mock terror. "He tried to *rape* me!"

Lee walked over to the campfire and looked at Rebecca. "No bow. She must've hidden it somewhere in the woods."

Melanie glared at Lee. "Bow? What are you talking about—"

Lee suddenly grabbed Melanie by the arm and roughly shook her. "Don't play games with us! You could've killed someone."

Melanie tried to pull free of Lee. "Kevin!" she shouted. "Are you going to let him do this to me?"

Kevin emitted a little snore, then opened a bloodshot eye. He moved uncomfortably on the ground, reached beneath his sizable rump and removed a bone he had been sitting on, tossed it into the campfire, and went back to sleep.

"Didn't Fletcher say something about us bonding, or some crap like that?" Cara asked nonchalantly, picking at her teeth.

Melanie jerked free of Lee and stumbled backward. Then she grabbed a smoking stick from the fire, its hot tip burning brightly, and charged at him.

Rebecca quickly karate-kicked the stick out of Melanie's hand. The potential eye-poker went spiraling into the night like a Chinese firecracker. But Melanie wasn't deterred. She went at Lee again, her sharp fingernails exposed like the claws of an angry cat.

Lee balled his hand into a fist and pulled it back. Melanie seemed to have second thoughts and stopped dead in her tracks, breathing heavily.

"Tsk, tsk, children," Brian said.

"So much for bonding," Cara snorted. "You want to tell us what happened, Spinelli? Or would you prefer to let your fists do the talking?"

"Seriously, cuz," Brian said. "What happened? Rebecca see a ghost again?"

"She tried to kill us is what happened!" Lee bellowed.

"I did not try to kill you!" Melanie shot back. "If I wanted to kill you I would have done it."

"So you admit to trying," Rebecca said.

"I don't admit to *anything*," Melanie said. "All I said is, if I'd wanted to kill you I could've done it."

"Why do you want to kill Lee and Rebecca, dearie?" Cara asked.

"How about the fact that he just tried to rape me," Melanie said.

"That's a bit after the fact, isn't it?" Brian asked.

Lee glared at Melanie, his jaw muscles clenching and unclenching. "Yeah, right! I tried to rape you the same way I tried to steal your car!"

A spark of life entered Brian's drunken eyes. He looked at Lee with a slightly befuddled look on his face. "You mean *this* is the girl whose car you stole?"

"I told you before I *didn't* steal her car. She set me up. And now she's trying to kill me. Me and Rebecca. Melanie flipped out when we broke up and she's been out to get me ever since. She's whacko!"

Suddenly, it all made sense to Rebecca. Melanie was the girl Cara had been talking about—the one who used to go out with Lee, the one Lee had beaten up . . .

Melanie was staring into the fire, chewing on her lower lip, her arms crossed in front of her. Then, suddenly, she broke into tears and ran into the woods.

Brian and Cara watched her, then looked at Lee. "You really know how to treat a lady, cuz." Brian said.

"Yeah," Cara said, but she said it to Rebecca.

Lee kept his eyes glued to Melanie until she disappeared into the woods. Then he turned to face Brian and Cara. "You two clowns think this is a big joke, but if she comes back here with that bow, you're going to find out this is no laughing matter."

"What is she, Robin Hood or something?" Brian asked.

"Close enough," Lee said.

"Who's Robin Hood?" Kevin asked, stirring from his

drunken slumber. He sat on the edge of the log and rubbed sleep from his eyes. "And who's Igor? Or did I dream that?"

"Jorge," Rebecca said. "He was some guy we caught snooping around in the woods tonight. He was spying on Cara and Brian when they . . . when they were down by the stream getting water."

"Does he work for Mr. Fletcher or something?" Kevin asked.

Lee shrugged. "We don't know. But just the fact that he's been hiding him from us is kind of suspicious, don't you think?"

Kevin shook his head dumbly. "I don't know."

"That's not all that's suspicious," Rebecca said. "I've been wondering how Fletcher's going to get all those campers over here from the mainland. There's just no way they're all going to fit into Martin's ferry. It almost sank just bringing the six of us over here."

"And what about *The Killing Game?*" Lee reminded her. "Didn't Fletcher say something about a killing game?"

"Yes," Rebecca said.

"Can you remember *exactly what* he said?" Brian asked.

Rebecca struggled with her memory. "He said . . . we are ready to *start* The Killing Game."

They all turned and looked up the hill, at the small gleaming dot of a house that twinkled like a star lost in a sea of blue sky.

"And what do you suppose he meant by that?" Cara asked.

Lee kept his eyes fixed on the house. "I don't know, but I'm going to find out." He looked at Rebecca. "Tomorrow night we're going back up there. And we're not coming back until we have some answers."

Fifteen

The next morning at the crack of dawn, Fletcher rousted them out of their tents. He gathered the sleepy-eyed group about him, including Melanie, who had returned some time during the night.

"Today is the final day of your training. You have done well, all of you, as I knew you would when I selected you to be my camp counselors."

He looked at each of them in turn. "I have tried to train you in three stages. First, I tried to teach you how to survive off the land. Second, I tried to teach you how to evade the enemy and how to defend your position, somewhat, through the use of mantraps. During the third part of your training, you will go on the offensive. Today, you will hunt each other!"

They stared back at Fletcher in silence as he dragged out a large wooden crate and deposited it at their feet.

"In the aftermath of a nuclear war we may find ourselves in a dog eat dog environment," Fletcher went on. "Where human animals must hunt one another in order to stay alive. Where only the strong will survive. Today, we will see who in our group is the strongest, who is the survivor. Today we will play *The Killing Game*."

Rebecca and Lee gave each other a knowing look as Fletcher pried open the wooden crate with the blade of his hunting knife. They peered curiously into the box. It was filled with jungle fatigue uniforms and boots and other gear. They looked at each other uneasily.

"Ah . . . Mr. Fletcher?" Lee asked. "Is this really necessary? I mean, you know . . . *hunting* each other?"

"Of course it's necessary, Lee," Fletcher said. "This is, after all, a *survival camp*. But don't worry, it's only a game. In fact, I think all of you will enjoy playing it. Now, please find a uniform that fits you and remove it from the box," Fletcher instructed them in a brisk voice. "There are also canteens and flashlights for each of you. Don't forget to fill your canteens with water before you break camp."

Fletcher smiled benevolently as they carried out his instructions.

"Without question the most difficult animal on earth to hunt is the human," Fletcher continued, his expression beatific. "The collective senses of the human being—good sight, excellent perception of color and depth, smell, hearing, taste—provides him with a hunting edge that is superior to any species."

At the bottom of the box were five menacing-looking pistols. Lee pulled one out. "What's this, Mr. Fletcher?"

Kevin answered for Fletcher. He removed a gun from the box and held it up. "Hey, Bri, air compression pistols!"

"Cool!" Brian replied enthusiastically, pulling a gun from the box and inspecting it. "We use these sometimes at the academy when we have war games. It shoots a paint-filled cartridge. If you get splattered with paint, you're dead."

Brian aimed the gun at Kevin who quickly dropped to the ground and pretended to retaliate with his own gun.

"A Zap war," Lee said, inspecting his gun. "I heard of them. I just thought I was too old to play them."

"You're never to old to learn how to survive," Fletcher said. "A mink raised in a cage that escapes to the wild is an easy animal to trap. But its wild cousin is as wily and cunning as any animal you will ever hunt. That's why we must train to return to our primitive roots."

Brian turned and fired off an imaginary shot at Lee. "You're dead, cuz."

Kevin leapt to his feet, swiveled, and fired off another imaginary shot at Brian, who dropped to the ground and rolled in true "gung ho" fashion.

"Kev, old boy, this is right up our alley," Brian said, firing back and then blowing make-believe smoke away the gun barrel. "I think it's about time we taught these civvies just what survival and war are all about."

Fletcher laughed heartily as Brian climbed to his feet and dusted himself off. "Excellent Brian, that's the spirit. Obviously you and your partner will have quite an advantage over the other two teams with your military background."

"Obviously," Brian agreed proudly.

Fletcher pointed to the thick woods that stretched out in all directions. "There will be three teams. Brian and Kevin, Cara and Melanie, and Rebecca and Lee. The woods before you will be your playground in this little game."

"Why not boy-girl teams?" Cara complained. "That seems more fair." She obviously wasn't too happy about having a screwball like Melanie as her partner.

"Because I believe in a real life situation this is how the six of you would pair off," Fletcher explained. "And—as an added incentive—I've decided to award the winning team a thousand dollar bonus at the end of the summer camp."

A thousand dollars! Now Rebecca was enthused.

Maybe a thousand dollars wasn't a big deal to two rich kids like Cara and Brian, Rebecca considered, but it sure was a lot of money to her and to Lee. Already she could feel the adrenaline begin to pump through her system. She wanted that money, and she was willing to kill to get it.

Well . . . sort of.

And yet, there were questions nagging at her that needed to be answered. "Mr. Fletcher?"

"Yes, Rebecca?"

"I was just wondering, when are the senior counselors arriving?"

"They will be arriving tonight by helicopter," Fletcher said.

"And the kids?" Rebecca asked. "When will they be arriving?"

"Tomorrow."

"Also by helicopter?" Rebecca asked.

"Or on Martin's ferry?" Lee asked.

"I'm renting a larger launch to bring them over," Fletcher said curtly. "I've dismissed Mr. Martin. His vessel is unseaworthy. Now, are there any more questions before we begin?"

Rebecca almost asked the question that had been on her mind when they had first arrived on the island: why he had hired them as counselors instead of kids who lived nearby. But she was intimidated by Fletcher and afraid her question might antagonize him. She remained silent.

When no one responded to Fletcher's question, he continued. "Good. Then let's get started. Eat breakfast and finish changing into your uniforms." He looked at his watch. "Meet me down by the dock at . . . 0800 hours."

Rebecca watched Fletcher limp away. He seemed to have all the answers. Maybe she had overreacted about The Killing Game. That's all it was, just a game. In fact, the possibility of making an extra thousand dollars was a pleasant surprise. The only puzzling detail remaining was—where did Jorge fit into this puzzle?

But Rebecca's enthusiasm for the game wasn't contagious. "Great," she heard Cara mutter. "Just what I wanted to do. Play Cowboys and Indians. Can someone just shoot me right now, please? I'd like to go swimming."

"Gladly," Brian said, aiming his pistol at Cara and pulling

THE KILLING GAME

the trigger of the empty gun. He twirled the gun around like an Old West gunfighter. "Before we start the game I'd like to congratulate the second place finisher—whoever you may be—on a war well fought."

"You're a real laugh riot," Cara said sarcastically. "But seriously, why don't we pretend one of us won and all go swimming? We can share the bonus money. That old codger with the gimpy leg won't know the difference."

Lee snorted. "That old codger with the gimpy leg's been leaving us panting for breath trying to keep up with him all week long."

"C'mon Cara, it'll be fun," Brian said, sighting down the barrel of his Zap gun. "You know how you like to get banged every now and then."

Cara turned red, then angry. "Will I get a chance to blast that stupid smirk off your face?" she asked Brian.

"You'll get a *chance*," Brian replied confidently. "But cashing in on it may present a problem." He spun around on his heel and aimed the gun at Rebecca's forehead.

"You're awful cocky," Rebecca said.

"He has reason to be," Kevin said, gazing at his fellow cadet with admiration. "He's the Hudson Military Academy's rapid-fire pistol shooting champion. He can put a bullet in a bug's ear with either hand."

"Thank you, Kev," Brian said beaming arrogantly, spinning the gun around like Billy the Kid. "I don't like to brag, but . . . let's just say I could probably also do it blindfolded."

Brian spun around again but this time, Lee's hand darted out to catch the barrel and snap the gun away. "You may be a real hotshot on the shooting range, but let's see what you do when someone's shooting back at you," he said, before handing the gun back to his cousin.

Rebecca watched Brian, his eyes a perverted measuring

stick for his true intentions, take careful aim at the back of Lee's head as Lee walked away.

If Brian's gun had been real, she might have screamed.

At exactly eight o'clock, Fletcher stood by the edge of the dock leaning on his rifle and chewing on a cigar stub as his counselor-warriors loaded their Zap guns.

Uncle Sam would've been proud of them. They looked like real soldiers dressed in their jungle fatigues and military gear. Rebecca recognized the rifle Fletcher was leaning on. It was the enormous one Lee had called the Weatherby.

"Treat these guns as if they were real weapons," Fletcher was saying. "But remember, a weapon by itself is not enough to defeat your enemy."

He grimaced as he leaned a little more heavily on his rifle. "I learned that very valuable lesson a few years ago, compliments of a rhino's horn. Believe me when I tell you—be smart! You've got to be cunning! You've got to be wily like the fox!"

Rebecca found herself nodding in agreement, even as her mind strayed elsewhere.

She recalled snatches of conversation she had heard around camp. Every one thought Fletcher was a bit of a kook; at the same time, they maintained a healthy respect for his skill as a hunter. He had surprised all of them on more than one occasion by sneaking up on them, appearing seemingly out of nowhere.

"You've got to use your head in the jungle. Use it or lose it," she thought she heard him say. She brought her attention back to reality. "Any questions?" he asked in his gruff voice.

"When is the game over?" Cara asked.

"When there is only one team left," Fletcher replied. "Or one player."

"Don't worry, Cara," Brian said confidently as he suddenly turned and shot a crab, splattering its shell a shiny red and sending it scampering back down the beach. "I'll send you swimming fairly early."

Cara made a face. "You may wish you hadn't—tonight."

"What if my . . . teammate . . . gets killed?" Melanie asked. She wasn't happy about having Cara as her partner, either, and made little attempt to hide it. "Will I get to keep all the money if I win?"

"Yes, you will," Fletcher said. "If your teammate is killed then you're on your own."

Cara held up her loaded pistol and examined it. It seemed big and out of place in her smallish hand. "Is this paint washable, by the way?" She looked down at her fatigues. "Never mind. I guess it doesn't matter with these rags."

"What's off limits, sir?" Kevin asked.

"My house and the north cliffs," Fletcher replied.

"Why the cliffs?" Cara asked.

"It's a nesting area for bats," Fletcher said. "I'd stay away from there if I were you. For your own good."

"Ugh," Cara said. "You don't have to warn me twice."

Fletcher took a fist full of straws from one of his pockets. He went from person to person and they each drew a straw. "The shorter straws will go first," Fletcher explained. "Then, I'll send you out at ten minute intervals—"

"You mean in teams, sir?" Lee asked.

"No," Fletcher said. "You'll have to hook up with your teammate in the woods. How you do it is your problem. But remember, if you chose to rendezvous someplace with your partner and your opponent guesses where that might be, then you're setting yourself up for an ambush. Is that clear?"

They all nodded.

Fletcher continued, "Each of you will start by heading north up the beach. Once you're around the bend and out of sight, you're on you own. Ten minutes each should give you enough time to scatter or take up a position. The game will officially begin in one hour. Synchronize your watches."

They synchronized the rugged jungle watches they had been issued as part of their gear. Lee edged up to Rebecca and whispered, "Meet me at the north cliff." She gave him a barely perceptible nod.

Cara drew the shortest straw and was the first to go, followed by Brian, Melanie, Lee, Kevin, and finally, Rebecca.

Rebecca's heartbeat quickened as her time neared. By then the woods would already be filled with enemies waiting to blast her.

But it was Melanie she feared the most. Would she ditch the Zap gun for a more lethal choice of weapon—like a bow and arrows?

Fletcher signaled her to go.

She would soon find out.

She jogged up the beach, cut into the woods as soon as she was around the bend, and circled back toward camp. She looked for a fallen tree that marked a barely distinguishable opening to a small trail.

It was a trail Lee had found while hiking around on his own. One that would take her very near to the north cliffs and to where, she hoped, Lee would be waiting for her.

She knew Lee was as curious as she was about the north cliff, that it was more than just a place to rendezvous. They had never hiked there during their training and Fletcher had specifically warned them away from it. She wondered why.

What was hidden there?

A shadow passed over her. Rebecca looked up and saw black clouds roiling across the clear blue sky. Then the air suddenly grew colder.

There was a storm on its way.

THE KILLING GAME

She heard a rustling in the tree branches above and a little behind her.

She froze on the path and went into a crouch, her heart hammering away.

Was there an enemy up there?

Hiding and waiting?

Drawing a bead on her with a Zap gun?

Or was there a more perilous danger lurking in the foliage?

Such as a bitter girl who wanted to use the back of Rebecca's skull as a bullseye for the lethal end of a very sharp arrow.

She dropped to the ground, turned, and fired.

Sixteen

What reflexes!

She cleanly had picked a squirrel off a tree branch with one well-placed shot.

Well, she never had been too crazy about squirrels, anyway. Just rats with furry tails. Furry *red* tails, now.

She continued down the small trail, which led east, away from the sun. Lee had told her the trail led to the eastern edge of the island where it turned north and ran to the cliffs. She stayed low and moved fast, her pistol held out in front of her, her ears alert to any unusual sounds or movements.

It was tough going through the thick foliage of the woods. Especially if she kept to the smaller, yet safer trail. It was the larger path where danger awaited, where ambushes were set. Low lying tree branches whipped into her face and brambles dug into her side.

She was relieved when she finally came to a small clearing. Her throat was parched and her fatigues clung to her skin, held there by a cold sweat.

She leaned against the smooth white bark of a tree trunk and uncapped her canteen. She held it to her lips and cool liquid slipped down her throat like a message from heaven.

The barely audible snap of a twig at the edge of the clearing rang in her ears like the report of a rifle shot.

She let instincts take over, honed sharp by a week of heavy

training, and without thinking, she dove to the ground and rolled away.

A splotch of red paint splattered against the tree trunk she had been leaning against. She came up firing in the direction of the shot and ducked for cover.

She heard sadistic laughter rip out of the woods. She couldn't tell if it belonged to a male or female. Rebecca peered through tall weeds but her eyes couldn't pick out her attacker. He or she was well camouflaged. Her only consolation was that she was just as well hidden.

She kept low and skirted the edge of the clearing. She started to make her way around the circle. Her intention was to come up behind her attacker. She ducked behind a thick tree trunk and ventured a peek around it.

She could vaguely make out the cold eye of a Zap gun's barrel poking through the underbrush. It was aimed directly at her! She ducked away and heard the soft thump of the zap gun followed by the whistling sound of a paint cartridge zipping past her brow.

She crouched down and swung out from behind the tree, got off two quick shots, turned and ran through the woods. She picked up the path and ran down it as if the devil himself were on her tail. She ran past fir and pine trees, moving as fast as she could, her limbs tingling with nervous energy.

"Aaaaaagh!" she roared, startling herself, almost overcome by the energy of the hunt. The Killing Game. She wondered, only briefly, somewhere back in the civilized portion of her mind, if she herself were becoming like an animal.

Like a wild pig.

And if this was what Fletcher had wanted.

If so, then he had gotten his wish. She carried in her hand a Zap gun. But she knew that if the gun were real, and if her life depended upon it, she wouldn't have hesitated to use it—she would've blown away anything in her path. And she would've done it with a smile on her face, and no guilt in her heart.

There were footsteps behind her, coming fast, hard, and heavy. She rounded a bend in the path, whirled around, hit the dirt, and waited. The gun butt felt cold and clammy in her hand. The footsteps grew louder. Her grip on the trigger grew tighter as she aimed the gun at the bend in the path.

The footsteps, crunching through dead leaves, were almost upon her.

She fired off three quick shots.

Birds screeched and flushed from the trees.

Her timing had been perfect.

She caught Kevin in the middle of his big barrel chest with all three shots. A nice, tight cluster. He didn't even get off one shot.

He didn't even know what had hit him!

Kevin stumbled in surprise and veered off the path, tripped over a low stump, and went sprawling head first into a thorny clump of bushes.

"Yes!" Rebecca screamed lustfully, Kevin's sadistic laugh now only a memory. "Laugh *that* off!"

She had done it, she had killed someone, and she had been thrown into ecstasy.

She turned and ran wildly. She didn't know how long she ran, or how far, but it was long enough and far enough to get her hopelessly lost in the wildest part of the woods.

Suddenly, the clouds thickened and covered the sky, making the dense woods almost as dark as night. The wind picked up and dead leaves swirled about her feet.

Where was she?

She looked up into the sky to gauge her direction. But the sun had disappeared behind the dark clouds.

She was lost.

She stood perfectly still, the thumping of her own heart

THE KILLING GAME

the only sound breaking the stillness of the woods. Then she heard it. The sound of salvation. There. Muffled but audible. The roar of cold ocean crashing against hard rock.

The cliffs.

There was one good thing about being on an island—the woods couldn't go on forever. Her momentary panic subsided. She wasn't lost. She knew she was bound to come to the coast if she kept moving in a straight line toward the sound of the sea. She heard it again, louder now, the rhythmic smashing of sea water. She was near, very near.

She pulled up short to catch her breath and take a drink from her canteen. She should have known something was funny when the birds all went quiet. The calm was oddly threatening.

The wind suddenly shifted direction. Then she heard another whoosh and out of the corner of her eye she saw it coming—the gleaming point of a deadly arrow tip, the lethal messenger of death glinting in the sunlight as it flashed before her eyes.

She shrieked as the canteen jumped from her hands as if tugged by an invisible string.

She looked down at the canteen with a stunned expression. The head of the arrow had punched a hole through the center of the canteen as easily as it would've punched a hole through the bone of her skull.

The Killing Game had taken on a grim, new meaning. She turned and ran for her life. The terrain sloped up, then down. Rebecca lost her balance and went flying, her hands frantically swiping at dead air as she tried to keep her body from tumbling down the steep incline.

She fell hard, hit a mound of dead pine needles with a thud, and started rolling down. She felt herself accelerating and clawed at the ground in a vain attempt to slow her descent. Finally, she crashed into the side of a fallen, birch tree.

Pain shot out of her bruised ribcage. She ignored it and scrambled to her feet. She would recover from a bruised ribcage, but an arrow through her heart might prove a bigger problem.

She looked around for her Zap gun, which had been ripped from her hand by her violent tumble down the hill, but saw it nowhere.

Then she realized how utterly useless a Zap gun would be against the lethal power of Melanie's bow and nearly laughed aloud at her own stupidity. The rules of The Killing Game had changed.

Rebecca gritted her teeth and made a mad dash up the opposite side of the steep incline, thinking that if the wind hadn't suddenly shifted when Melanie shot her arrow, it might well be her *head* rather than a canteen leaking.

Her hand tore at an exposed root and she pulled herself over the rim of the incline. She dove into a clump of tall ferns and lay there catching her breath. She listened. Nothing. Listened some more. Still nothing. She must've lost her. Lucky for her, since Melanie was as good a runner as an archer.

She bounced to her feet and ran to the ocean, her chest heaving as she sucked up badly needed air. She reached the rim of the cliff and leaned against a pine tree.

She had to stop and take a breath before her heart exploded from exertion. Her ribs hurt more than ever, now. She longed for a cool drink of water and reached for her canteen before she remembered it lay punctured in the dirt, a victim of Melanie's arrow.

An arrow whistled through the air and thudded into the tree trunk inches above her head.

She ducked down, thankful now for all the hard training Fletcher had put them through. Her physical conditioning was probably the only thing keeping her alive.

THE KILLING GAME 149

She felt a fresh surge of energy. She pushed off the tree and ran down a path that rimmed the cliffs. To the left, the path snaked up into a craggy cluster of rocks; to the right, it led down to a long expanse of open beach and the sea.

She quickly debated her options. The cliffs might offer cover from Melanie's rain of malignant arrows—but they might also be a dead end. Or worse, Lee could be up there waiting for her and she would lead Melanie right to him.

But where there was a beach there was water. And she was a good swimmer. But could she swim far enough or quickly enough out to sea before Melanie could draw a bead on her?

There was only one way to find out.

She took the path to the right and ran. She didn't get very far. Just around the first bend she stopped so suddenly she nearly gave herself whiplash. Directly in front of her, staring balefully at her through bloodshot eyes, was a peccary—a wild pig.

They had seen a few while hiking around the island, usually just the pigs' hind quarters as the animals ran from the humans' trampling feet. Now, Rebecca was looking one of the ugly creatures right in the eye.

It had two frightful tusks jutting from a jaw that belonged to a face—if you could call it that covered with rubbery warts. The pig was the size of a pitbull but twice as ugly; it looked three times as fierce.

She turned and ran back up the path toward the cliffs. She would take her chances up there. She ran even harder now, her heart thumping away in her chest, her arms churning at her sides as her feet thudded along the ridge path.

Ahead of her the cliffs loomed—and something else. Two things she couldn't quite make out with her naked eye. They moved liked two huge moths, two indistinct shadows zigzagging frantically, outlined against an angry sky that threatened to burst open as the storm grew closer and closer.

Her eyes briefly followed the fluttering shadows until they disappeared behind a cluster of rocks up there on the small plateau.

The sun briefly poked out from beneath a heavy layer of low gray clouds.

Rebecca raised her eyes to the rocks again. Just before the sun disappeared, she saw it. The opening to a cave. She hurried up the path to where the cave awaited her like a hungry mouth, dark and ominous, ready to devour her. With some trepidation, she peered inside.

It was hard to gauge the depth of the cave—no way to tell what might be in there waiting for her. She looked over her shoulder for Melanie, but saw no one. She looked back into the cave. If she had wanted to hide, this would be as good a place as any.

She wondered if Lee had felt the same way. "Lee?" she called in as loud a voice as she dared. The exploding waves drowned out her voice.

She took a few steps inside the cave. "Lee?" she called a little louder, her voice echoing off the dense cave walls. She walked in a few more feet and gazed into the darkness. She pulled her flashlight from her utility belt and flicked it on.

She nearly swallowed her heart when the beam of light struck Brian directly in the face.

Seventeen

Brian flinched from the light but the Zap gun in his hand remained steady and true. It was aimed right at her heart. His shadow did an eerie dance on the cave wall behind them as he raised the gun and aimed it squarely at her forehead.

She flinched as she awaited the air compression paint pellet to come ricocheting off her skull.

Brian flicked on his own flashlight and held it beneath his chin, the light giving his face a macabre look. "Good evening," he said in a low and spooky voice. He was clearly enjoying himself. Then his expression grew stern. "You want to get that light out of my eyes before I paint your forehead red?"

She snapped off her flashlight but before the yellow cone of light had faded completely, she thought she saw a flicker of movement deep in the recesses of the cave. Maybe it was only the way the light had reflected off the cold, stone wall.

"Where's your gun?" Brian asked, before she had time to think about it any farther.

"I lost it in the woods."

Brian looked at her suspiciously. "You wouldn't be trying to hide it from me, would you?"

"No."

He took a few steps until he was standing just inches from her. "I may have to frisk you."

"Do it and you'll eat that gun." She was tempted to feed it to him anyway. Brian was basically a rich wimp with a well practiced smirk. Rebecca was pretty confident she could take him in a fight. The only thing that prevented her from wiping the stupid sneer clean off his face was the thousand-dollar bonus Fletcher had dangled in front of them.

"Oooooo," Brian said in mock terror. "You are so *bad.*" He took a couple of steps back, the tone of his voice becoming more businesslike. "Well, I was going to offer you a deal. But not if you're some sort of woman's libber."

"What sort of deal?"

"Guess."

Rebecca gritted her teeth. "Cara not *girl* enough for you?"

"She's too much, really. Sometimes I just wish she'd leave me alone."

"You're just a spoiled little rich boy, Brian."

Brian raised his eyebrows questioningly. "Not even for a thousand dollars?"

"I'd die first."

"Okay," Brian said with a disappointed shrug, aiming the gun between her eyes and squeezing the trigger.

"Wait!" Rebecca cried. "Forget about the stupid game for a minute."

"Stupid?" Brian scoffed. "There's nothing stupid about a thousand dollars. Father taught me that at a very young age."

"I think Melanie is trying to kill me!"

"Of course she is, so am I, so are we all. It's The Killing Game—"

"I mean *for real.*"

Brian lowered the gun momentarily. "Didn't we go through all this last night?"

"She tried to kill me *just now!*" Rebecca exclaimed. "Five minutes ago!"

"Did you see her?"

Rebecca paused. "No."

"Did you see her last night?"

"No," Rebecca said, without pause this time. "But someone's shooting arrows at me. And she's a champion archer."

"How do you know that?"

"Lee told me."

Brian smirked. "He would."

"He told me on the ride to the ferry, before any of this happened. Do you think it's just a coincidence that someone on the island is shooting arrows with deadly accuracy?"

"If she were shooting arrows with deadly accuracy you'd be dead now, wouldn't you?" Brian shrugged. "Like I said, it's your word against hers."

"Look . . ." Rebecca searched for the words to make Brian understand that his life and everyone else's was in danger. Melanie belonged in a lunatic asylum, not on an island with Lee and the rest of them. And certainly not on an island with a bunch of innocent little kids.

Maybe Fletcher would deal with Melanie, because one thing was for sure, Rebecca wasn't going to step out of the cave until Melanie was safely put away. If Melanie were staying, then she'd have to go. She'd get off this island, one way or the other, even if she had to swim all the way back to the mainland.

"All right, kill me," she said. "But afterward would you *please* tell Fletcher I think Melanie is trying to kill me and Lee."

"Well, thanks for the invitation," Brian said, aiming the gun at her face again. "But I was going to kill you anyway. I'll leave it up to you to enlighten Fletcher with your strange fantasy. I have a game to play."

Rebecca froze. She could see it now, whatever it was, creeping through the murk.

Coming toward them.

It was right behind Brian.

Eighteen

Now it was Brian's turn to freeze. Then he slowly lowered his Zap gun.

"When you want to shoot—shoot—don't talk." Lee flicked on his flashlight. Then he reached around Brian and ripped the Zap gun out of his hand before roughly pushing him forward. "I didn't like the way you propositioned Rebecca," he said angrily.

"All in jest, Lee," Brian said, forcing a pleasant smile as he turned to face his cousin.

Lee looked at Rebecca. "Sorry for letting it go on as long as I did, Rebecca, but I had to wait and see if Kevin was bringing up the rear."

"We don't have to worry about Kevin," Rebecca said. "I shot him."

Brian was irate. "Kevin let you kill him?"

Rebecca was indignant. "He didn't *let* me kill him. I shot him fair and square."

Brian shook his head in disappointment. "Disgraceful. An Academy man letting a girl put him away . . . I got Cara, by the way. Shot her when she went for a dip. I don't know if Melanie's still in the game, though."

"Melanie's playing her own version of The Killing Game," Lee said, his voice tinged with irony.

Brian looked at Lee. "When did you join our little party, by the way? I didn't see you come in."

"I was here already, you dork, waiting for Rebecca. We're all in this cave for the same reason—Fletcher told us to stay away from it."

"That's not why I'm here, cuz," Brian said. "I'm here because I knew you two would come here and it seemed like a good place to set up an ambush. I even had my man Kevin staked out in the woods near here to pick you off if I didn't get you. Of course, the moron screwed up royally and got himself killed. What I can't understand is how *you* got here ahead of me."

"I know a shortcut," Lee said. "While you and Cara were down by the stream fetching water, I was scoping out the island. Checking out all the trails Fletcher *didn't* show us."

"And why were you doing that, cuz? Don't you get enough exercise during the day?"

"Why do you think I did it? In case I had to get the hell away from Melanie." Lee looked at Rebecca, an apology in his eyes. "I didn't think she'd go after you."

"You both seem pretty sure little Miss Melanie is at the bottom of all this," Brian said.

"Why would I lie?"

"To get revenge on her for testifying against you in juvenile court?" Brian asked with raised eyebrows.

"Revenge?" Lee spat out. "I don't want to have anything to do with Melanie anymore. I just wish she'd go away. But forget about Melanie for a minute. I think we have an even bigger problem."

"You're so full of intrigue, cuz."

"I was thinking a lot about Fletcher as I sat here in the dark, watching you sit here in the dark. There's something screwy about that guy."

"No kidding," Brian snorted. "Tell me something I don't already know."

"I mean seriously screwy. First of all, there's that guy Fletcher neglected to tell us about running around the island. Jorge. What's the deal with him? You have to admit, that's pretty strange."

Brian nodded in agreement.

"And last night," Rebecca broke in. "Lee and I did a little snooping around in Fletcher's house. You know, the house that's *off limits* to us. Well, the walls are decorated with photos of all these animals he's killed, and there is a room full of weapons. I mean, it's like Camelot in there!"

"And have you noticed there's no way off this island?" Lee asked. "Unless you can swim thirty miles. I haven't seen a boat since Martin dropped us off. It's like we're trapped here."

"So what's your point?" Brian asked.

"Our point is this," Rebecca said. "Something's going on here, and it's got nothing to do with a summer camp."

"So don't keep me in suspense. What is it all about?" Brian said.

"We don't know—yet," Lee answered. "But when we find out, we want you on our side. And I figure if we get your help, then Kevin comes along with the package. Am I right?"

"That's correct, cuz. He does what I tell him to do. He'd better. I'm paying him more than Fletcher is. So, let's say I believe you, that Fletcher is up to something. What are we supposed to do about it?"

"Tonight, when the senior counselors arrive, I say we go in the house again. Do a little snooping around," Lee said. "Check things out."

"We? You mean me, too?" Brian asked, a little nervously.

"I know you won't believe a word I say till you see it for yourself," Lee said.

"And what if things don't check out?" Brian asked. The crack in his nerves was growing wider.

"Then we'd better find a way to get ourselves off this island," Lee said grimly.

"And what do *I* get out of it?" Brian asked suspiciously.

"You mean besides your life?" Rebecca asked.

"We'll let you win the stupid game, how about that?" Lee suggested.

Rebecca jumped when Lee suddenly shot her in the butt with the Zap gun. Then Lee turned the gun on himself, splattering paint all over his belly button.

Brian looked stunned. "You just let me win? Just like that?"

"All we ask for is a little cooperation on your part when the time is right." He handed Brian back his Zap gun. "And, of course, you'll have to take care of Melanie. I don't mean just shoot her with a stupid paint gun. I want either you or Kevin to follow her everywhere she goes. Rebecca and I don't need to be looking over our shoulders every two seconds."

"And if you see her with a bow in her hands, wrap it around her neck," Rebecca said.

"I'll even throw this into the deal," Lee said. "I won't tell all your friends at the Academy what a chicken you were the first night on the island. Remember? When your Academy brother was swinging around from his heel? I won't tell them how you came running down that hill, screaming like a girl—"

"Hey!" Rebecca said.

"Sorry," Lee said quickly.

Brian smiled bleakly. He walked over to the cave entrance and peered out. Then he turned and gave them both a little salute with the barrel of his gun. "Tonight, cuz. We'll party to celebrate my victory."

THE KILLING GAME

Brian disappeared into the twilight outside the cave. Lee shone his flashlight along the cave wall until the cone of light fell upon a small hole near the back wall of the cave. It looked just large enough to crawl through.

Lee got down on his hands and knees and shone the light into the black opening. The beam of the light barely penetrated the thick gloom of an inner cavern.

Rebecca thought she heard a faint rustling sound coming from inside the dark hole.

"Well," Lee said, pulling his head out of the opening. "Can't see much this way. Let's go on in and take a look around."

Rebecca nodded reluctantly. Lee led off and she followed him through the hole. A minute or so later they were standing up inside a cavern so dark, the black in front of them seemed to stretch out to infinity.

Their two flashlights threw out bright, criss-crossing cones of yellow light. Rebecca spotted it first. About thirty yards away she saw what appeared to be a solid wooden door.

She pointed it out to Lee and they made their way toward it. The cave floor felt soft and mushy beneath their jungle boots. Then she heard it again. A gentle rustling sound. Then they both heard it. It came from above them. They aimed their flashlights upward.

First, they saw a dim light at the top of the cave, probably caused by an opening large enough to let in a little daylight. Rebecca strained her eyes but could see no way to reach the opening.

Then, it seemed as if the walls of the cave up there were moving. As if they were alive!

Suddenly, dark shadows began to drop from the cave roof, followed by a massive, piercing screech. The air in the cave came alive with flying, furry things. Bats! The bright light must have panicked them.

Rebecca threw her hand up and screamed as the first wave of bats descended upon them. She felt the flapping of their wings and saw their little, red glowing eyes only inches away from her face.

There must have been hundreds, maybe thousands of them reflected in the twin beams of light. One landed on Lee's back and stuck. Rebecca knocked it off with her flashlight. It flew screaming into the darkness.

The swarm was nearly smothering them. Rebecca fell to her knees. A bat landed on her head and tried to sink its talons into the long tangles of her blond hair. Lee swatted it away with the barrel of his Zap gun.

Shrill screeches hissed throughout the blackness as the bats continued to pummel them. Then came a shrill, terror-filled wail. It took a moment for Rebecca to recognize that particular sound.

It was her own scream of horror.

Then she heard the soft *thump, thump, thump* of Lee's Zap gun and the air was filled with red paint.

"Follow me!" Lee screamed, his voice nearly hysterical. He grabbed Rebecca's hand and they made a run for the door in the cave wall. A red splattered path was laid down in front of them as Lee shot the Zap gun.

Finally, the gun clicked on empty. Lee tossed it aside, grasped the metal ring on the door, and pulled on it with all his might.

His muscular biceps were bulging nearly to the breaking point before the door finally creaked open. He shoved Rebecca through and quickly followed, pulling the door shut behind him.

She was still swatting away invisible bats until Lee gently took her flailing hands and pulled her to him. "It's all right, we're safe now."

She collapsed into Lee and sobbed. "They were everywhere, Lee, everywhere! In my face, my hair—"

"I know, I know," Lee said soothingly, running his hand through her long blond hair. "But it's all right now. They're gone."

Rebecca allowed herself one more sob before collecting her wits and wiping away her embarrassment with her tears. She was acting like a frightened little girl instead of a trained warrior. She unwrapped herself from Lee and inspected her surroundings.

They were in some kind of a tunnel.

She shone her flashlight down a winding corridor; Lee had dropped his at the door of the bat cave. The beam of light illuminated a narrow tunnel stretching out before them. It was made of dirt, held up by ancient, rotting beams of wood every twenty paces or so.

"Let's check it out," Lee said, giving her a nudge. "Unless you want to go back the way we came."

She shuddered, fought back her revulsion, and made her way down the tunnel, a single cone of light leading the way. Rebecca shivered slightly in the cool damp air. Her knees felt wobbly and she reached out her hand to steady herself on the earthen wall, dislodging a large clump of dirt.

"Be careful where you put your hands," Lee cautioned. "Or you might bury us alive."

Rebecca felt a sudden chill of alarm. Lee had a way with words *guaranteed* to make her uneasy. It didn't help any, either, when her flashlight suddenly flickered and went out.

"Whoa!" Lee shouted, bumping into her from behind. "What happened?" They were standing in pitch blackness. Rebecca flicked the switch on and off—nothing. "Cheap army surplus flashlight, I guess," Lee said.

Rebecca fought back the panic creeping up from the base

of her spine. She tapped the flashlight with her hand. The light came back on, weak and wavering.

The thin cone of yellow light illuminated a giant bug. Caught in the spotlight, it looked enormous and threatening. It had at least a thousand legs, and used every one of them to disappear quickly inside the folds of a rotten wooden beam.

"What was that?" Rebecca asked.

"I don't know," Lee said, looking around. "But the place is literally crawling with them. Come on," he said, giving her a little push. "Let's go on while we still have some light. The opening can't be much further."

The tunnel curved to the right and started to slope down. Rebecca picked up her pace as the light grew a paler shade of yellow. She could smell the ocean now.

"There's probably a way out down by the beach," Lee said.

"What do you think this tunnel was built for?" Rebecca asked.

"My guess is that there used to be a lot of bootlegging along the New England coast during prohibition. The bootleggers probably used this island. It wouldn't surprise me to learn that Fletcher's grandfather was right in the middle of the whole scheme. The bootleggers probably brought their boats right up on the beach and smuggled the booze through the tunnel to the cave, where they hid it."

"With all those bats back there?"

"They probably used torches to keep the little creatures away," Lee speculated. "I mean, if you wanted to keep nosy people away from your booty, what better place to hide your caché, right?"

Rebecca didn't answer him because the flashlight beam sputtered and went out again, throwing them once again into inky blackness. The dark snugness of the tunnel was an echo chamber for her heartbeat. Then, it came back to her like a kick in the face; that dizzy feeling, hot and nauseous.

"Feel that?" came Lee's voice from the blackness.

A current of cool, salty air, ever so slight, curled up around her feet and revitalized her.

"It's a draft of air. We have to be close to the ocean," she heard Lee say.

He squeezed past her. The tunnel was so tight their chests brushed together. Under different circumstances, Rebecca might have enjoyed this moment. But it was hard to think of romance when you were trying not to vomit.

She felt Lee's hand grope for hers. He pulled her along with him until the tunnel got wider and they saw four bright cracks of yellow, the outline of a doorway.

They crept up to it. The current of air was stronger now, more pungent with the smell of the ocean. They heard muffled voices from behind the door arguing loudly.

"I told you to stay out of sight!" It was Fletcher's voice.

"I did!" The voice that answered spoke with an accent.

"I overheard the girl, Cara, whispering something to her boyfriend about a tall, skinny guy, spying on them down by the stream. It was you, wasn't it?"

There was a pause. "It was so hot in this little room that I *had* to go out for air. It is like staying in a closet in here—"

"Stay away from their camp—"

"I did, I was down by the stream—"

"Don't go anywhere near them!" Fletcher yelled. "They're suspicious enough as it is. Especially, Rebecca and Lee. I can see it in their eyes. They've already found my weapons room. I found one of my arrows stuck in the front door of the house this morning."

"I'm sorry, Eduardo."

"I want everything to go off without a hitch tomorrow. I brought you here to do a job, not to go sightseeing. Keep your nocturnal wanderings to the vicinity of the north cliffs, Jorge."

"*Sí*, Eduardo."

"Until The Killing Game is over."

Nineteen

There was a moment of silence as Rebecca and Lee stood spellbound. Then, Fletcher began to speak in a kinder, gentler tone of voice. They put their ears to the door so as to not miss a word.

"You're a gifted young man, Jorge. The collectors of the unusual will pay amazingly high prices for prizes such as these. Even more for a younger specimen."

"Thank you, Eduardo. And then, when you sell the island, we will be rich, no?"

"We'll be rich enough."

"And then we can leave this pig island?" Jorge asked. "The wild pigs frighten me and it gets so cold on this island, at night."

"Yes, dear boy," Fletcher said affectionately. "Then we can leave the island."

Rebecca squatted and peeked through the keyhole. Fletcher was running his hands through Jorge's long, dark hair like someone petting a cat. She felt as if she were peeking into someone else's nightmare.

"And return to the jungle?" Jorge asked hopefully, turning his blind eye toward Fletcher. "Where it is warm?"

"We will return to the jungle where it is warm and live like kings," Fletcher said, giving the young man's shoulders a reassuring squeeze. "Kings of the jungle. Like Tarzan and his Boy."

"Who is this *Tarzan?*"

"Never mind."

Jorge grew petulant. "Do I have to stay in my room again tonight?" He rose from his chair and out of her line of vision. "I get so bored when I'm all alone."

"No, not tonight," Fletcher said, taking the seat Jorge had vacated. His broad back obliterated her view. "Tonight I want you to meet the others. After all, we don't want *you* getting shot by mistake, do we?"

They laughed.

"Perhaps we should leave now, in fact," Fletcher said. "It's getting dark out and our guests will be arriving soon."

"*Sí*, Eduardo."

Fletcher rose from his chair and snuffed the lantern that sat on the table in front of them. The room went dim. Then Rebecca heard a door being locked and pulled her eye from the keyhole.

"Well . . . that was informative," Lee said.

"Can we get out of this tunnel before I suffocate?"

"Right," Lee said. He gave the door a push but it wouldn't budge. He put his shoulder to the door and pushed harder, but it still wouldn't move. Rebecca helped, and they pushed for all they were worth, before finally giving up.

"It must be locked," Lee said.

"Great. *Now* what do we do?" Rebecca asked, looking back down the long dark tunnel.

"Hey—what's that?" Lee asked, pointing to her chest.

"Lee!" Rebecca said curtly, expecting him to flick her nose. She was in no joking mood.

Lee's eyes were wide and gleaming in the dark tunnel. "For real . . . the key."

She looked down and could see the key glowing in the dark, actually *glowing* a luminous yellow. She quickly removed it from her neck before it burned a hole in her chest and slipped it into the keyhole. The rusty lock tumblers rasped then clicked into place as she turned the key.

They put their shoulders to the door again and pushed. The door still wouldn't move. They tried again, huffing from the effort.

The door, protesting noisily, creaked open.

They stood at the threshold, staring into the dark room. It stank of sweat and something else, a chemical, medicinal smell Rebecca couldn't identify. They stepped cautiously into the room.

Lee felt his way across the room, unlocked and opened the other door, and then the shuttered window. Rebecca spotted a book of matches on a wooden table next to the lantern, lit it, and the room came alive with an eerie glow.

Through the opened window and door they saw a cloudy, blood-red sky as the sun dipped toward the horizon. Rebecca turned the lantern up a notch.

The room was small, bare except for a cot, an ice chest, and a sturdy wooden worktable that was covered by a thin sheet of Plexiglas. Tools of a trade that neither Rebecca nor Lee recognized were resting upon the worktable, next to a small, buckskin bag.

Rebecca hefted the bag. There was something in there roughly the weight and size of an orange. She untied the rawhide cord that bound the soft leathery bag and emptied out its contents.

Breath hissed out of their mouths as they gasped in horror.

A shriveled, shrunken head bumped across the table top. Lee slowly reached down and picked up the tiny head by its long, gray hair, exposing a miniature face set in rough, leathery skin.

A wave of nausea swept over Rebecca.

The head and features had been excellently preserved. The long, straight nose had a pinched look to it and the eye sockets had been sewn shut with small, precise stitches. The lips were also sewn shut, but with a thicker, wider cord, leaving the death mask with a permanent frown.

Even so, Rebecca recognized the face. She had seen it in a photograph. It was Edward Fletcher's father.

Twenty

Rebecca's heart was pounding so hard it was painful. She gasped for air in the hot, stuffy little room. She thought she might faint.

Lee quickly returned the head to the bag and came to her side. "I know, I know," he said quietly, wrapping an arm around her. "I recognized him from the photo." She could tell that Lee's heart was beating as heavily as hers was and found this oddly reassuring.

Lee left her side to extinguish the lantern. They walked out of the little shack carved into the side of the cliff and locked up after themselves. The sun was finishing its dip now, and they felt the delicious tickle of a chilly, refreshing sea breeze.

The beach was a short distance away. Both of them took off running. They dove into water as cold as ice and swam a short distance out.

Rebecca wanted to keep swimming until she reached the mainland. But if exhaustion didn't kill her, the frigid water might. She and Lee swam back to the beach, and fell to the sand breathing hard.

"He's mad. The guy's gone totally off his rocker," Lee said. He stifled a hysterical laugh. "He's going to shrink our heads!"

"We have to tell the others," Rebecca managed to utter. "And then, we have to get off this island."

A steady drizzle began to fall. The wind whipped over the beach, pressing the tall grass of the dunes nearly to the ground. Lee looked up as gray clouds blotted out the stars. "A storm's on the way."

Then they heard a low, thumping sound from above them. They looked up and saw a helicopter descending from the sky, lights blinking and flashing. It flew directly over them before disappearing over the tree tops. It was headed south, toward Fletcher's house.

"They're here," Rebecca said.

"Let's go," Lee said. "We haven't much time." They jogged all the way down the coast line in the steady drizzle until they reached the dock where Martin's ferry had dropped them off only a week ago. To Rebecca it seemed like several lifetimes had elapsed since she first set foot on this cursed island. She and Lee made their way to the encampment where despite the rain, a party was already in progress.

"I'd like to propose a toast to the winner . . ." Brian was saying as Rebecca and Lee entered the camp. Four sets of eyes turned to face them as they made their way over to the flickering campfire, fighting to stay alive as the steady drizzle of rain grew thicker.

"Hey, the other losers," Kevin said. "Just in time to join our little celebration."

"We were just toasting the winner of The Killing Game," Brian said. "Melanie Anderson!" They all raised tin cups to their lips—Rebecca guessed those cups didn't hold water—and drank heartily.

Rebecca shot a look at Brian, who only shrugged, a chagrined expression on his face. "She got me right outside the cave," he said.

Then Rebecca looked at Melanie, who was smiling that mysterious smile of hers, and it took all of her willpower not

THE KILLING GAME

to walk over to her and pluck her head right off her shoulders. But they had other, more pressing problems to attend to first.

Kevin had his arm around Melanie, and both of them appeared to be drunk. He offered the tin cup of booze to Lee. "C'mon," he coaxed. "Let's be friends. We may as well. We're going to be spending the next two months together on this island."

Lee refused the tin. "Yeah," Brian said. "Lighten up you two. We made it through our first week and The Killing Game is over. Let's celebrate a little."

"The Killing Game is *not* over," Lee said. "It's just about to begin."

"Come again, cuz?" Brian asked, staggering a little. Tonight, like every other night, he had been putting away the booze like there was no tomorrow.

"The senior counselors flew in tonight," Rebecca said. "By helicopter. They flew over us as we were coming up the beach. We think . . . we think . . ." The taste of the truth was so acrid it nearly choked her.

Lee finished for her. "We think they're here to *hunt us.*"

"We are *The Killing Game,"* Rebecca said.

They were met with a stunned silence. Then Cara gave a little laugh. "What?"

"We think they're here to hunt us for our heads. They're going to shrink them and sell them," Rebecca said. She wished there had been another way to say it. She knew how absurd it must sound to them, and it didn't surprise her when they laughed.

"What have you guys been smoking?" Cara asked. Melanie and Kevin slipped away into the shadows.

"I know it sounds incredible, but it's going to happen. Probably tomorrow morning. There *are* no campers coming later. There *are* no senior counselors. We think they're hunters. And we think they're here to hunt us."

"Yeah, right," Brian broke in. "And Melanie was running around in the woods with a bow and arrow like Robin Hood. Well, all I can say is, she shot me fair and square—with a Zap gun. I didn't see any bow and arrow. Right Mel . . ."

Melanie and Kevin were over by the log locked in a tight embrace. Kevin was nuzzling Melanie's neck, and Melanie was looking over his shoulder at Lee. Brian chuckled before turning his attention to Cara.

"C'mon Cara," he said. "Let's go do some celebrating of our own."

Cara took a drink from the tin and emitted a little giggle. "You mean in the rain?"

Brian took Cara's nearly empty tin and tossed the contents into the fire. The flames licked up, then down again. "Why not?" Brian asked. "Animals do it that way."

Then Brian kissed Cara forcefully and she returned it with a passion that was purely animal. Their kiss didn't seem out of place in the mud and the rain and the dying flames of this weird and spooky island.

Lee took Rebecca by the arm and led her away from the revelry. "C'mon," he said in a low voice. "They couldn't help us if they wanted to."

She turned to Lee. "Where are we going?"

"Into the house."

Twenty-one

Lee grabbed a flashlight from his tent and fresh batteries for Rebecca's and they hurried up the hill. As they approached the hunting lodge, they could see the banquet hall was alive with light and noise.

They circled around the house to the back door of the kitchen, which was open a crack. The smell of roasting pig invaded their nostrils. They crept up to the door and peered in.

Jorge was popping a bottle of champagne. Near him sat a tray with eight empty glasses. He placed the bottle on the tray and whistling merrily, scurried out of the kitchen through twin swinging doors. As the doors swung open, Rebecca and Lee heard laughter from the banquet hall.

"Ready?" Lee asked in a taut whisper. Rebecca nodded. He pulled the back door open and they snuck inside. They made their way over to the swinging doors and opened them a crack.

There were six newcomers in all, and Jorge was handing each his or her glass of champagne. When everyone had their drink he placed the tray down on the banquet table, next to the carved up pig, and took a glass of champagne for himself.

"A toast," Fletcher said, holding up his glass.

The group held up their glasses.

"To the hunt," Fletcher said.

"To the hunt!" they all bellowed merrily.

"To The Killing Game," Fletcher said, downing his champagne.

"The Killing Game!"

They drank their champagne.

Rebecca and Lee watched as Fletcher's eyes fell upon a short, fat, middle-aged woman with dark hair tied in a severe bun. She wore the standard khaki garb of a safari hunter, as did the rest of them. "Jan," Fletcher said, "have you and your husband ever hunted in the Amazon River Basin?"

Jan smiled and glanced at the man seated next to her. "Can't say that we have, Ed."

"You must pay Jorge and me a visit down there some time. The Jivaro Indians are the masters at hunting humans."

Rebecca turned her gaze to Jan's husband. He was a mountainous man with a thick neck and a square heavy jaw clamped around a short stubby pipe. Gray hair peeked out from beneath a sweat-stained bush hat. Tiny blue eyes, as hard as nails, darted about the banquet hall.

"Think you might be interested, Pete?" Fletcher asked Jan's husband.

Pete puffed on his pipe. "Not at these prices, mate."

Both Jan and Pete spoke with heavy accents. Rebecca guessed they were Australian.

An evil smile stretched across Fletcher's face. "I think I can give you the jungle discount rate next time."

"Does that apply to me as well, *Monsieur* Fletcher?" a broad shouldered man asked, his mouth full of roasted pig. His lips were thick and smacking. His dark hair receded on a domed forehead above equally dark eyes.

"I was in the Amazon once, years ago," the man was saying. "The Jivaro Indians served as my guide. Why, did you know that the Jivaros are the only people in the world that can track a man by smell? By *smell!*" he repeated for emphasis.

"And the Somalis, Bernard," Fletcher corrected him.

"Really, *Monsieur?* I did not know that. Are you sure?"

"*Mais oui,* Bernard," Fletcher said. "I hired them myself as trackers when I was a mercenary in their country."

"Do you think, in a fair fight, they would be a match for the Jivaros?" Bernard asked.

"In a fair fight they might, but the Jivaros never fight fair," Fletcher laughed. "That's why I admire them so."

"Did they serve as your guide as well, *Monsieur?* In the Amazon?" Bernard asked.

"They do now," Fletcher said. "After they killed my best man with the Jivaro Catapult, I thought I'd better have them on my side. That's a wicked little mantrap. Have you ever run across one, Bernard?"

"No, *Monsieur,* I can't say that I have."

"No one I know has either," Fletcher said. "And lived to tell about it. If you return to the Amazon, have one of the Jivaros show it to you."

"I look forward to the experience," Bernard said with a twinkle in his eyes.

"And I to this one," a man with an Italian accent said. "It's costing me enough. For what you charge, Fletcher, I could've bought a new Ferrari."

"You were never under any obligation to pay the price, Paolo," Fletcher reminded the Italian man. "But I think after the hunt, the rarest of hunts, you will have found your *lira* well spent. A bargain for the money, in fact. These are fine young specimens—fast and strong."

And so the conversation went for the better part of an hour as the group exchanged safari stories and hunting tips. Rebecca and Lee stood transfixed near the opened kitchen door, peeking into the banquet hall when they dared, just listening the rest of the time.

Besides Jan, Peter, Bernard, and Paolo, there was a thin,

scholarly looking man they called Chris who spoke with an English accent. And a tall, willowy blond with refined, arrogant features set in a head that seemed too large for the rest of her body. They called her Heidi.

Six hunters.

Six rich hunters from all reaches of the world.

One for each of them.

Twenty-two

Rebecca fought off a sick feeling in the pit of her stomach. She had been afraid before, but not like this. Her whole body quivered with tension and she felt weak all over, as if her legs would no longer support her. Her arms felt numb and tingly like they had fallen asleep and were now just waking up.

It was thundering and the light drizzle had turned into a heavy, steady rain. But the storm outside was no match for the storm inside Rebecca's head.

"How do we know they will cooperate, mate?" Peter asked.

Fletcher chuckled wickedly. "I have come up with an ingenious little plan to ensure their participation. I have told them that you are senior counselors in a summer survival camp, and that you are going to hunt them with air compression guns—paint pistols—as part of their training."

This brought on gales of laugher.

"Or, they may catch you in a snare trap, like a rabbit," Fletcher said, and this brought on more laughter. "I've taught them how to make a few basic mantraps, for a little added amusement."

"And what if one of these chaps traps us or *kills* us with one of these paint pistols?" Chris asked, his voice full of mirth. Myopic eyes stared back at Fletcher through thick lenses as he awaited the answer.

"Then you must return to the hunting lodge at once," Fletcher said. "And I will hunt your game."

This brought on a round of protests. Lee cracked the door a little wider so they could take a better look. The protests were cut short when the hunters saw the look in Fletcher's eye.

Rebecca saw it, too, and what she saw caused a chill to run up her spine.

Fletcher's face was lit with an unholy leer; his eyes burned like two hot coals. "Without danger there is no game," Fletcher said with a quivering lip. "If you die, be thankful that your death is only a symbolic one, and not the real thing, which I can also provide. At no added cost," he added looking at Paolo.

Looking at him now, there was no doubt in Rebecca's mind that Edward Fletcher was totally insane.

The next thing Rebecca knew, Jorge was walking toward the kitchen with a tray of dirty dishes.

Lee closed the door and looked frantically about. They had to hide fast! Rebecca saw a small closet and jumped into it, pulling Lee in behind her.

It was a cramped, smelly little space. Rebecca felt something hot and sticky rubbing against her shoulder. She tensed. The smell was horrible, whatever it was. She felt a twitch in her nose and fought off the urge to sneeze.

They could hear Jorge fussing around in the kitchen, then, all was quiet. Lee cautiously opened the door a crack. The kitchen was deserted. Dirty dishes and pig bones were piled high in the sink.

They bolted from the closet and Rebecca glanced over her shoulder. She had been leaning against a stinking, wet mop; the noxious smell of it still clung to her nostrils.

Then she sneezed.

They froze as they heard Fletcher's voice. "I will show

you to your rooms, now," he was saying. Good, he hadn't heard her. "Get a good night's sleep, The Killing Game will begin tomorrow at dawn."

The Killing Game. The very thought of it made Rebecca's blood run cold.

"If you bag your game," Fletcher was saying, "return to the lodge at once with the carcass and turn it over to Jorge. And remember—no head shots!"

The banquet hall buzzed with excitement as chairs rustled and thanks were given to their gracious host. Good nights were exchanged, then the voices and footsteps dwindled to nothingness until all was quiet in the banquet hall.

Rebecca's eyes connected with Lee's and held them. Their worst fears had been realized. "So . . . what are we going to do now?"

Lee gave the question some serious thought. Finally, he said, "Well, we can run, or we can fight."

"Run where?" Rebecca asked. "We're on an island. They're bound to hunt us down sooner or later. And it's too far to swim to the mainland."

"Don't forget about the helicopter."

"You can fly a helicopter?"

Lee made a sour face. "No, of course not. But whoever flew it here can. We could hijack it. If it's still here. And it probably is. I didn't hear it take off. Would you take it up in this kind of weather? We could *make* the pilot take us to the mainland. If we're lucky, we can get back here with the police before Fletcher's even discovered we're missing."

"If the pilot works for Fletcher he's probably armed. How are we supposed to hijack this helicopter?" she asked. "With a Zap gun?"

"What, are you kidding? There's a whole room full of weapons in this house!" Lee exclaimed. "Let's go get some."

Rebecca could feel her heart beating loud and hard. She

opened the swinging door a little. The banquet hall was dark, deserted. Laughter drifted down from the floor above. She closed the door again.

Lee registered her reluctance and tried to be more persuasive. "So . . . what do you say?" Lee asked. "If we have to fight them, we'll lose. We don't stand much of a chance against six well-armed hunters. Not with Zap guns and hunting knives. If we had that Weatherby it might even things up a bit."

Rebecca said nothing. What *could* she say? The thought of killing another human being had never crossed her mind before. Why should it? She was from Cooper Hollow, a sleepy little town in the Hudson Valley, where the big excitement was illegal drag racing down Old Wilson Highway late at night, when the adults were asleep.

"Don't you think?" came Lee's voice again. The voice of reality. Horrible reality.

"We still wouldn't stand much of chance. They're veteran hunters."

"Yeah, right," Lee scoffed. "Fletcher might be, but those others . . . c'mon. They probably sit in a blind somewhere sipping tea and eating crumpets while the natives do all the work."

Rebecca still wasn't convinced. "I say if the hijacking plan doesn't work, we hit them with a preemptive strike," Lee went on. It took a moment for the shocking clarity of the statement to stick in her consciousness.

"You mean . . . kill them in their beds?" She felt weak in her legs and light in her head. Just the thought of it, of sneaking into their rooms at night and slitting their throats, the cut jugulars spurting crimson, the death cries lost in a bloody gurgle. She knew she didn't have the guts to do it.

"It's either that or let them track us down and shoot us like wild pigs," Lee was saying. "I don't know about you, but I don't think the apple-in-the-mouth look is for me. Or my head on some sick, rich guy's knick-knack shelf."

Rebecca forced a weak smile. She looked at Lee, who was looking back at her in anticipation. "Okay. Let's do it," she croaked, and pushed open the door.

They ran across the banquet hall floor, then down the main corridor to the smaller corridor that led to the weapons room.

With a trembling hand she removed the skeleton key from her neck and inserted it into the keyhole. She unlocked the door and they entered the room. Silently, she closed the door behind them. Lee snapped on the flashlight and shone the beam of light on the gun rack.

The rifles were gone.

"Damn," Lee muttered. "That was our best bet. Fletcher must've gotten suspicious when he found the arrow stuck in the door." He removed an ancient crossbow from the wall and tucked it under his shoulder. "Better than nothing, I suppose."

They had no sooner left the room when they heard footsteps and Fletcher's voice. They instantly dropped to the padded carpet like trained commandos.

"Remind me to talk to Martin about the boating accident," Fletcher was saying. "We need to find a place where the current is strong enough to carry a body out to sea."

"But, Eduardo . . ." It was Jorge. "Won't six headless bodies floating out to sea arouse suspicions?"

Fletcher and Jorge walked past them, heading for Fletcher's room.

"That's just a cover-up, a story to give the authorities until the sale of the island is complete. We'll bury the bodies here, perhaps in the cave beneath the bat guano," Fletcher said with a chuckle. "Even if they do launch an investigation we'll be miles away by then, back in the jungle . . ."

Their voices faded away. Or maybe Rebecca just didn't

want to hear anymore. She had heard enough, more than enough. Her percolating blood led to a grim resolve and she knew, now, that she would do what she had to do.

"I miss the jungle," was the last thing she heard Jorge say before the two men entered Fletcher's room. Well, she would send him back to it. Six feet under.

"C'mon," Lee said, scrambling to his feet. "Let's get the hell out of here. We have work to do."

With only a crossbow and two hunting knives, they ventured out into the night like two avenging angels. The rain had stopped, leaving the air hot and wet, hard to breath, like the air inside a sauna.

Then they heard it. An engine cough and catch, then a high whining sound. Lee turned his head in the direction of the noise. "It's the helicopter—it's leaving the island!"

They ran to the clearing in time to see the chopper lift off the ground in a whir of wet whooshing air and flashing lights. Lee dropped the crossbow and ran after it. He leapt and managed to get a hand around the slick pontoon. He held on desperately as the chopper rose into the air.

Lee struggled to maintain his grip but to no avail. His hand slipped and he fell back to the earth. He hit the ground with a sickening thud before rolling over several times.

Rebecca, her heart slamming inside her chest, ran over to where Lee lay in a twisted heap, and rolled him over on his back. "Lee?"

Lee didn't answer her.

"Lee?"

Lee still didn't move.

"Lee!"

But Lee was dead.

Twenty-three

"Lee!" Rebecca cried.

She was answered with chirping insects and tree frogs. A deafening symphony contrasted to Lee's silent, inert form, still and cold on the hard wet ground. The front of his camouflage jungle shirt had torn open, and beneath it she could see his rock n' roll T-shirt.

The Grateful Dead.

"Lee . . ." she pleaded. "Don't leave me all alone on this awful island—please!"

This was supposed to be a fun summer, Rebecca thought bitterly. A chance to make some good money. A chance to do something different instead of drudge work like waitressing or working in the mall. Well, it was different, all right. "I want to get out of here!" she cried suddenly, overcome with fear she could no longer hold back.

She didn't realize how hard she was squeezing Lee's hand until he pulled it away. His lids rolled up to reveal pain-filled eyes. Then, he slowly stirred to life and sat up. "Man," he moaned, "I feel like one big bruise."

Rebecca felt a little foolish. She wrapped an arm around Lee's thin, tapered waist to help hold him up until he got his legs back. She could feel his taut stomach muscles, as hard as rock, beneath his camouflaged clothing. His long, ebony hair framed his head in a tangled mess.

Lee flexed his muscles to bring new life to them and his

eyes took on a grim, determined look. He turned his face to the sky and watched the chopper disappear into the night, little more than a blinking dot now.

Lee's somber expression turned into a deadly sneer. "He saw me, that guy, the pilot. He saw me hanging there and he took off anyway. He didn't care if I fell or not. He's going to pay for that. Somehow, someday, he's going to pay. They all are." His voice dripped with bloodlust. His intensity scared Rebecca. He sounded as insane as Fletcher.

"We'd better go warn the others," Rebecca said, hoping to get Lee's mind off revenge and back to their predicament.

"I guess you're right," Lee said, standing on his own now. "Although they didn't exactly buy it last time. Still, I guess we should try again."

"Melanie, too?"

Lee gritted his teeth, a vein in his temple twitching madly. "Yeah, Melanie, too."

They stashed the crossbow in some nearby bushes. "Lee, what really happened between you and Melanie? Can we really trust her? I'd feel a lot better if I knew the whole story."

With a resigned sigh, Lee told her everything. "Melanie and I used to go together. Since about sixth grade, actually. It was the sort of thing you just assume will last forever. At least, Melanie assumed that.

"I guess she thought we'd get married some day, have kids and play softball with them on the weekends, grow old and get fat, the whole bit. But then we broke up a few months ago and she totally lost it.

"Her car was in the shop at the time, at the garage where I worked. She asked me to do her one last favor and return her car when it was ready. But on the way to her house, the cops pulled me over.

"She had reported the car stolen, and she stuck to the lie when they took me to court. I probably would've gotten off with a suspended sentence, but when they found me guilty, I guess I was the one who lost it. I went over to her house, took a tire iron to her car and made a real mess of it.

"I got to admit it felt pretty good at the time. Every time I smashed that iron into her car, I imagined I was smashing her face. But then I got expelled from school, lost my job . . ." Lee shook his head in disgust. "Unbelievable. She set me up, and now we're trying to save her life."

"You still want her on our side?"

"Yeah," Lee said, his tone softening a little. "Because I have to admit, now that I've had some time to think about it, that I was a real jerk about the way I broke up with her. I . . . I was kind of a chicken, I guess. I called her up and blew her off on the phone. After all those years together I didn't even have the decency to tell her to her face. The way I handled the whole thing definitely sucked. Being on this island with no TV or other stupid distractions has given me a lot of time to think. And I think maybe we were both wrong."

"Did you ever hit Melanie?" Rebecca asked, tentatively.

Lee stopped and looked at Rebecca, stunned. "Of course not. I lost my temper and all—I mean I wanted to hit her, but I didn't actually do it."

They walked the rest of the way in silence. When they reached the campground, they found it wet and deserted. Then they heard a soft sobbing sound. It came from Brian and Kevin's tent. Lee walked over to it and whipped open the tent flap. He shone the light inside.

The cone of light picked up Melanie's face staring back at them with eyes that were two dark pools. Blood dripped from her lip, which she wiped away with the sleeve of her camouflage shirt. On top of a sleeping bag, a short distance away, Kevin snored drunkenly, with his pants down around his ankles.

"What happened?" Lee asked gently, stepping into the tent.

"I guess things got a little rough," Melanie said, choking back a sob. Then her face muscles quivered and she lost it all together. "He tried to rape me but thank goodness he was too drunk to do it . . ." Lee took Melanie into his arms.

Rebecca stepped away from the tent flap to give them some privacy. Still, she could hear a little of what was going on inside. "The others helped," she heard Melanie say.

"You mean Cara and Brian?" Lee asked.

"Yeah," Melanie said, her voice now coming in sobbing gasps. "They held me down. I thought it was a game at first. They were kidding me because I'd won the Zap gun war. But then—then they got carried away."

"Animals," Rebecca muttered to herself. The cloud cover broke in the sky above her. Through the mist she was captured in the luminous glare of a full and unforgiving moon.

Then she heard Lee explaining the situation to Melanie in a hushed voice, explaining to a girl who nearly had been raped, that she had an even bigger problem, now. A few minutes passed, then Lee and Melanie stepped out of the tent.

"It's The Killing Game for real," Rebecca said when Melanie looked at her, as if to leave no room for doubt.

"What . . . what are you going to do?" Melanie asked.

Rebecca turned and looked up the hill. For the first time since they'd been on the island, the house was throbbing with life. The windows glowed and occasionally laughter drifted their way on the breeze. Rebecca hated Fletcher and his hunters. They had become her enemies with a capital E. "We're going to go up there and get them first."

Melanie stared back at her with eyes that were bewildered and also wild with excitement. "Are you sure?"

"We're sure," Lee said. "They're not going to slaughter us like so many deer. We're going to fight back. Even if they ultimately win, I plan to take a few of those bastards with me. Are you with us?"

Melanie's answer was simple enough. "I'll go get the bow."

"So . . . you *were* the one shooting at us?" Rebecca said.

Melanie looked down at her feet. "Yeah," she said in a quiet voice. "And the snake and . . ." She looked up at Rebecca with a mischievous grin. *"Rebeccaaa . . ."* Then she almost started crying again. "I really am sorry. I wasn't trying to kill you. I just wanted to scare you—"

"It worked!" Rebecca said, remembering how terrified she had been in the hunting lodge the night she heard the eerie whispering of her name, and then later when she felt at the mercy of Melanie's deadly arrows.

"We'd better hurry. Melanie, get that bow and every arrow you have," Lee ordered. "And meet us around the back of the house, by the kitchen door." Melanie nodded and dashed off.

Lee went to his tent. He retrieved his survival book and stuffed it into his back pocket. He looked up the hill at Fletcher's house, his eyes burning brightly. "I don't know what those creeps paid Fletcher for this little hunting expedition, but he better hope their checks have cleared because some of those chumps aren't going to be around to pay off after this little game is over."

"What about the others?" Rebecca asked, "Cara, Brian, and Kevin?" She wrapped a piece of rope around her waist.

"What about them?"

That was all he said, and that was all he had to say. Rebecca had once tried to convince them of the mortal danger that faced them all, but their answer had been a laugh in her face. Now, especially after what they had done to Melanie, she knew Lee didn't care about what happened to Cara, Brian, and Kevin.

Nor did she, she realized.

They headed back up the hill, grimly resolved to do what had to be done. They veered off onto a side trail and Lee slid his hunting knife out of its sheath. The razor sharp blade gleamed in the moonlight. "Look for some sturdy branches, dry ones if you can find them."

"How big?" Rebecca asked.

"About the size of an arrow," Lee said, a grim reminder to Rebecca of the crossbow stashed in the bushes.

A quick search found several such branches, which they snapped off and took with them. Back at the clearing, Lee retrieved the crossbow and they made some quick calculations. Then they whittled the branches into arrows to fit the bow. Lee stood up, making the point on the last arrow needle-sharp.

The survival book fell out of his back pocket.

Suddenly, the wind whipped up hard and whistled through the tree tops, blowing away what little cloud cover remained. The moon shown brighter than ever. It was as if someone had suddenly flicked on a night light over the entire island.

The pages of the survival book started to flip rapidly, blown by the wind. The flipping stopped as suddenly as it had begun, and the book skidded across the wet grass, as if pushed by some invisible hand. It stopped at Lee's feet.

Rebecca felt a wave of goose bumps sweep across her body.

Lee picked up the book. It had opened to a mantrap called the Leg Breaker. It was a fairly simple booby trap that Fletcher had neglected to tell them about. The trap consisted of rubbing grease or some other slippery substance on a smooth log or rock. When the enemy stepped on it, he slipped and, if you were lucky, broke his leg.

Lee closed the book and shoved it deep into his shirt, not trusting it to his back pocket. His face was slightly befuddled as he grabbed the homemade arrows. They made their way back to the house. The kitchen lights were on and the back door was cracked open. Cooling on the wet grass outside the back door was a steaming bucket of bacon grease.

Melanie was nowhere in sight.

They both looked at the bucket of bacon grease, and then at each other, a knowing look in their eye.

The Leg Breaker.

Lee looked around. "Do you see Melanie?"

"No."

Lee breathed out heavily, a look of profound disappointment crossing his face. "Maybe she got cold feet, or . . . panicked." Lee loaded a makeshift arrow into the crossbow with a trembling hand. "Can't say that I blame her." He gave Rebecca a quick kiss. "Ready?"

She nodded, her heart slamming into her ribs.

The Killing Game was about to begin.

Lee cranked the ancient crossbow as tight as he could get it and pushed the kitchen door open. "Let's try to get Fletcher first," he whispered in a barely audible voice. Rebecca, close to hyperventilating, could only nod her reply. They entered the kitchen.

They were confronted with the sight of Jorge suddenly entering from the other direction, a tray of dirty dishes in his hand and an apron wrapped about his waist. Jorge stared at them, his eyes wide with confusion.

Rebecca and Lee, momentarily paralyzed by Jorge's sudden appearance, stared back mutely.

Then Rebecca heard a sharp twang.

Lee had fired the crossbow.

Twenty-four

The arrow shot through the air. Maybe it was because Lee's hand was trembling, but the arrow missed Jorge by inches, and punched a hole through the refrigerator door. For an ancient bow, it still packed some wallop. Lee fumbled to reload the bow.

Jorge got over his confusion in a hurry. An arrow aimed at your chest could do that to a person. Before Lee could fire again, Jorge was running back through the banquet hall, back to Fletcher's room, his terrified scream echoing off the walls.

Rebecca pulled out her hunting knife and went after Jorge. She caught up to him a dozen feet from Fletcher's bedroom door but before she could drag him down, the door abruptly opened and the leader of the pack himself limped out, naked except for a bathrobe hanging limply about his large girth. Rebecca was tempted to plunge her hunting knife as far into Fletcher's dirty heart as it would go.

And she would have, too, if he hadn't reached around the door jam and brought out the Weatherby. By the time he got it to his shoulder she was already running back into the banquet hall. She ran into Lee on the way out, running toward her, cranking up the crossbow.

"Did you get him?" Lee asked, his breath coming in hard gasps.

"Yeah," Rebecca snarled. "But not soon enough. Fletcher saw me and he has the Weatherby."

"So much for that idea," Lee said bitterly. "Now all hell is going to break loose."

They had to get out of there. A crossbow and two hunting knives were no match for a Weatherby. As they ran out of the house, Rebecca glanced over her shoulder and saw lights flashing on all over the hunting lodge.

Fletcher was rousting the hunters from their beds.

There would be no waiting for dawn, now.

"Lee," she said. "We can't just leave the others at the campground to die, no matter what they did or how we feel about them. It would be a turkey shoot; they wouldn't stand a chance. And Melanie's still out there somewhere."

Lee considered what she said. She knew what he was thinking: that they didn't have time to spare; every second was crucial; they had a small chance to live, at least for one more night, if they made a run for it *now*. That chance would grow a lot smaller if they took time to warn the others.

Rebecca watched the gamut of emotions run across Lee's dark face in that long moment. "Okay—let's give it a try," he said at last, swallowing hard.

Rebecca grabbed the bucket of grease and they tore across the clearing back to the house, back to where the hunters at this very moment were slipping into their gear and loading their rifles. Loading their rifles with bullets that had the names of the Cooper Hollow kids written all over them.

There was no time to take the back trails now, not if they wanted to beat the hunters to the camp. That meant running past the hunting lodge to get to the main trail. Lee was cranking the bow up even tighter now as they ran across the clearing.

With his attention diverted he hadn't seen the big fat one, the Australian called Peter. He was hiding in the darkness of the doorwell just waiting for them. Hiding in the murk as he lined Lee up in the cross hairs of his hunting rifle. Hiding in the gloom as he waited to bag the first trophy.

But Rebecca had seen him. "Lee!" she screamed, giving Lee a hard push. He stumbled and fell, somehow managing not to lose his grip on the crossbow. Then she saw the fat one aiming the gun at her guts and she hit the ground.

The gun barked death in her direction, spouting a fiery flame from the rifle barrel. Now Lee had seen his target. He went into a crouch and carefully aimed the crossbow at the fat Australian, taking plenty of time to get it right this time, and giving silent thanks that it wasn't the skinny one named Chris he had to hit.

His hands weren't trembling now as he squeezed off an arrow.

The fat Australian had the trigger of his rifle half-squeezed when the bow string twanged and death, in the form of a hand-carved wooden shaft, plunged into his soft chest and drove him back into Fletcher's door with the force of a pile driver.

Then the rain began again.

It came down harder than before. A glorious, purifying rain. It was like a sign from heaven, Rebecca thought. Or maybe from hell. But either way, she knew deep in her heart that someone or something had sent that rain to wash away the carnage that she and Lee would leave in their wake that night.

Because there was going to be a blood bath. In fact—she looked at the fat Australian, stuck to Fletcher's door like an insect on display—it had already begun.

The door opened and a short, fat woman came into Rebecca's view. It was Jan, the Australian's wife, and she was greeted with a rather gruesome sight. Her eyes filled with sadness when she saw her husband skewered to the door.

Then something else flickered in her expression. Rebecca recognized the look of fear. Jan knew that the tables had turned—the hunted had become the hunters. This was a different game than the one she and the others had in mind when they put down their money and signed up for this expedition.

Lee quickly fired off another arrow. Jan must have heard it coming, because she threw up her hands as if to ward off the projectile. The arrow ripped through her right hand before punching through her left eye and part way through the back of her skull. It sent a spray of blood splashing across her dead husband's face as she fell in a heap beside him in the doorway.

Then the Italian one, the one called Paolo was standing over her, a rifle in his hands. He saw Lee reloading and ducked behind the door.

"They'll pick us off easy if we try to get down the main path now," Lee said. "Let's try to lead them away from the campground. Maybe the gunshots alerted the others, or maybe Melanie warned them."

Somehow, Rebecca doubted that. They ran toward the woods and melted into the shadows. They found a small trail that led to the cliffs behind Fletcher's house and hurried down it.

Behind them Paolo crashed through the woods. A shot rang out and a bullet whistled through the air and tore through a pine cone just inches from their faces. They ran for the cliffs and squeezed between two large rocks.

Lee loaded another arrow into the crossbow. They had only one more arrow left. Rebecca looked over the side of the cliff. Beneath them, a cluster of particularly jagged rocks jutted out of the cliff side like razor sharp tombstones. They couldn't go that way. And if they went the other way, Paolo would pick them off.

From their hiding place they saw Paolo coming. Lee rose up, took aim, and fired off another arrow. Paolo, a little more agile than the fat Australians, hit the ground before the arrow hit him.

"Dump that stuff," Lee said, indicating the bucket of bacon grease that Rebecca still lugged with her as he loaded the last arrow into the crossbow. She dumped the gooey substance on the rocks they had just run over as Lee cranked the bow as tight as he could get it.

Lee rose up, but this time Paolo was waiting for them, with his eye to an infrared scope. From a prone position he fired off a shot. A red dot appeared from the barrel followed by the loud crack and the crossbow seemed to disintegrate even as Lee pulled the trigger.

The arrow flew harmlessly into the dark, blue night. Then Lee was falling backward with a handful of splinters. He pulled the biggest one out with his teeth and they turned and ran, leaping from rock to rock.

They could hear Paolo's footsteps thudding down the path to the rock where they had hidden. They saw his head appear and then the rest of his body was outlined against the moon as he climbed onto the rock.

Paolo put his gun to his shoulder and took one step forward to set himself properly. It was the last step he would ever take. His feet slipped out from beneath him and he and the gun went sailing over the side of the cliff, accompanied by an agonizing scream.

Rebecca and Lee ran to the edge of the cliff and looked down. It was an appalling sight. Paolo lay smashed on the rocks like a ruptured bag of raw hamburger, his cracked rifle a few feet away. "Damn," Lee said, pulling another splinter out of his raw and bloody hands with his teeth. "I wanted that rifle. Rebecca, do you think you could climb down there and get his ammo belt?"

"I'll try," she said, looking down the side of the cliff.

"Bring up the rifle, too, there may be something we can salvage. Hurry!"

Rebecca unlooped the rope and tied one end around her waist. Lee tied the other end around his waist. "Good luck," he said as Rebecca went over the side.

It was about thirty feet down to the body, and the closer she got the more gruesome it was. The rocks around the body were slick with blood and the smell of ruptured entrails was already attracting the gulls.

Rebecca tried not to look at the thing that used to be Paolo as she pulled off his ammo belt and grabbed the rifle. She tugged on the rope and Lee pulled her back up.

When she got to the top she noticed that Lee had ripped up his Grateful Dead T-shirt and had part of it wrapped around his bloody hands. His jungle shirt was off, too, and even in this moment of crisis, Lee's body took her breath away.

Lee checked out the rifle as she relooped the rope. Finding it useless, he took it by the barrel and smashed it against the rocks. The scope broke loose, and he jammed it into his waistband. He slipped his jungle shirt back on and draped his body with the gun belt. The survival book, which had been stuffed in his shirt, lay on the ground at their feet. The wind whipped up and flipped through the pages of the book. And then, it stopped.

Shivers ran up and down Rebecca's spine as she picked up the book to see which mantrap the ghostly forces of the island had chosen for them. Lee watched with curious, bewildered eyes.

The Jivaro Catapult.

She recalled that Fletcher and the Frenchman Bernard had been discussing this mantrap earlier during their dinner of roasted pig and champagne. Lee looked over her shoulder and they read the description of the trap together—basically a tightly wound band that held and swung a spiked paddle. The band could be made of rope, which was strung from a tree root stretching up to an overhanging tree branch. The paddle was held back under tension by a thin trigger stick, which was tied to a trip wire that crossed the victim's path. When the wire was tripped the spiked paddle swung around and impaled its victim.

"Well . . ." Rebecca said. "I have the rope."

"And I know where we can get a spiked paddle, or the next best thing," Lee said. "C'mon."

They took the twisting path around the cliff side down to the lagoon. From there, they made their way up the beach to the old, dilapidated dock to which Martin's ferry had been moored. Lee handed her the gunbelt and waded into the water. He poked around beneath the dock until he found what he wanted. Then he slammed his palm up and under a loose plank and drove the board upward.

Rebecca could see immediately what he was up to. She ran the length of the dock and yanked the board free of the rotting pier, rusty nails and all. It would be perfect for the Jivaro Catapult.

That's when they heard gunshots echoing through the night.

Lee pulled himself out of the water and draped the gun belts back around his chest. "Those gunshots came from the camp," he said, a desperate edge in his voice. Rebecca steeled herself. The others could be dying at that moment. She took a deep breath and silently prayed that they were all right.

The gunshots came again, shockingly brutal in the still of the night.

Lee grabbed the plank, careful not to drive a rusty nail through his already wounded hands, and they started off in the direction of the camp.

They stayed low and when they got to the fringe of the

camp they hid in a clump of bushes. The rain was still pounding down, steady and true. It pelted off the only tent that had a light shining from inside it—Brian and Kevin's tent.

They heard more gunshots. These came from the direction of the stream. *The Killing Game* was in full swing, and the prey were running for their life. Now they know, Rebecca thought, now they know. She wondered if that deadly knowledge would be of any use to them now, or was it too late.

When it seemed safe, they made their way over to Kevin's tent and pulled back the flaps, peered inside.

Kevin was still in there, and his pants were still down around his ankles.

But Kevin wasn't sleeping anymore.

There was a bloody, bubbling hole blown in Kevin's back, big enough to throw a football through. The walls of the tent were washed with a crimson red.

They had shot him as he slept.

Twenty-five

Not very sporting, Rebecca thought morbidly, as she swallowed back the bile creeping up in her throat.

Gunshots rang out, making them jump. They were a little farther away this time. "They're driving them to the north side of the island. They'll have them trapped there," Lee said with hate-filled eyes.

They made their way to the stream with their hearts slamming inside their chests and hid in the same place they had hid the night before when they caught Jorge spying on Cara and Brian. But there was no one there now. The stream gurgled angrily past them as more gunshots cracked through the night air.

"I don't see anyone," Lee whispered. "Maybe we should fill our canteens now that we have the chance. We may not get one later."

Rebecca nodded her agreement and crept over to the bank of the stream. They filled their canteens and it wasn't until they were recapping them that they saw the grisly image.

The bodies were floating downstream like two waterlogged, rotten tree trunks. They were tied together, entwined in death as they had been for much of their lives—Cara and Brian. A large furry river rat had already made a home in Cara's frizzy red hair, and it seemed to be giving them the evil eye as the bodies floated past.

Rebecca recoiled in horror and it took all of her will power not to scream. As they climbed back up the bank of the stream, more gunshots reverberated in the night air.

"It must be Melanie. She's still out there somewhere," Lee said. He attached his canteen to his belt and picked up the spiked plank.

"What do we do now, Lee?" Rebecca asked, searching his eyes. But there were no answers there.

Lee shrugged as if all the weight of the world sat on his broad shoulders. "I don't know . . . I don't know," was all he could mumble. "Do you have any ideas?"

Rebecca looked north, in the direction of the gunshots. "I say we head for the bat caves."

Lee wasn't sure if he had heard right. "You're sure that's what you want to do?"

"Melanie followed me there when we were having our Zap gun war. I think if she can, she'll try to make it back there and hope we do the same. Even if she's . . . even if she doesn't make it, we might be able to hide there. For one night at least."

Lee couldn't argue with her logic. They made their way upstream a little before finding the twisting trail through the woods that led to the north cliffs.

They reached the spot where Rebecca had nailed Kevin earlier in the Zap gun war. Lee pulled up next to a gnarly, rooted tree and leaned the plank against it. "This is as good a place as any," Lee said.

"For what?"

"For the Jivaro Catapult."

"What about Melanie? She could walk into it, too."

"We'll have to keep an eye on the trap and dismantle it before we leave," Lee said. "Unless . . . until . . ." Unless or until we nail someone with it, Rebecca thought, completing his sentence. Or, until we find Melanie dead.

They went about rigging the trap, the two of them working

feverishly to complete it before they were discovered. Lee tripped the contraption with a stick to test it and the plank with the rusty nails whipped out of the foliage and into the path like a spinning top. It slammed into the tree trunk with a brutal force that shook leaves from the tree.

Lee pried the board loose from the tree trunk and reset the trap, a grim smile sneaking across his face. He looked at Rebecca. "If it works half as well on a human body as it did on that tree, then I think we're in business . . ." His voice suddenly trailed off as Lee looked over her shoulder, his eyes filled with alarm.

Rebecca shot a glance over her shoulder and saw a man standing in the path, a pistol in his hand. It was the Englishman, the scholarly-looking one called Chris, except he didn't look so scholarly in his blood-spattered safari jacket. They had been so intent on setting their trap they had let their guard down briefly, but those few moments had been long enough to allow the hunter to sneak up on them.

She recognized the pistol. Lee had pointed it out to her in the weapons room. It was an odd looking weapon with a long barrel—a Remington XP-100.

"Excellent job setting that trap, sport," the Englishman said. He turned the gun on Rebecca. "Be a good little girl and remove that hunting knife from its sheath, would you?"

Rebecca removed her hunting knife and let it drop to the ground. The Englishman's eyes returned to the mantrap. "Jivaro Catapult, isn't it?"

He took a few steps closer to get a better look. "Yes, I believe it is," the Englishman commented. "The trap Fletcher described to Bernard earlier tonight. Gruesome little piece of work." He chuckled lightly. "It certainly isn't to snare a rabbit, is it?"

"Why don't you step into it to find out, creep!" Lee snarled.

THE KILLING GAME

The Englishman drilled Lee with staring eyes. He exuded the aura of power that came with being on the right side of a gun. "I have a better idea, sport," he said. "Why don't you step into it?"

Lee's eyes drifted to his knife, now jammed into the tree trunk. The Englishman followed Lee's gaze away from him to the knife, and that's when Lee made his move.

The Englishman must have anticipated Lee's move. He had plenty of time to turn the pistol on Lee and squeeze off a shot. The bullet hit Lee squarely in the gut and spun him around. He fell face down in a muddy puddle and lay perfectly still at Rebecca's feet.

Rebecca, numb with shock, stared down at Lee.

The Englishman motioned her away with the barrel of his gun. She took a few steps back as the Englishman knelt before Lee and rolled his body over.

Lee spat a mouthful of mud into his face. The Englishman, momentarily blinded, staggered back and reached up to yank off his muddied glasses. Then Rebecca heard a familiar click and the gleaming blade of Lee's switchblade came flashing through the air in a deadly arc. The knife slammed into the Englishman's thigh right up to the hilt.

Then Lee fell back into the puddle, too weak to do much more as the dazed Englishman staggered backward, shrieking in pain. Unfortunately, he had managed to keep his grip on the pistol.

He aimed the gun at Lee's heart and Rebecca lunged for it. He was distracted only momentarily, just long enough to hit her on the side of her head with the long barrel of the funny-looking pistol. She fell to the ground, rolled over, and looked up.

She saw him aiming the pistol directly between her eyes.

Twenty-six

Rebecca stared up at him, willing him to stop.

He paused, as if her thoughts had influenced him.

Remember . . . no head shots, Fletcher had said, and the Englishman must have remembered those words because he lowered the gun to her chest and cocked the hammer. The skull pendant about Rebecca's neck started to glow fiercely and he paused a second time.

Rebecca looked up into the man's face and saw twin skulls reflected in his eyes.

The second hesitation proved to be the fatal one, because death came screaming out of the night in the form of a barbed arrow. The tip of the barb tore through the back of the Englishman's neck, punching a dark hole through the front where his Adam's apple had once been. He fell to his knees, a wash of scarlet filling his mouth. Then, his face hit the ground. He lay there choking to death on his own blood. Once he tried to get up, but only managed to roll over, snapping off the feathers of the arrow. Then he lay still again.

Rebecca stood on shaky legs and saw Melanie running down the path toward her with a bow in her hands. She paused when she saw Rebecca and gave a little wave.

Rebecca waved back.

Then a shot rang out and Melanie pitched forward. She stumbled a few feet before falling, but Rebecca knew she was probably dead before she hit the ground.

Rebecca had no time to mourn the death of the girl who had just saved her life—she had two more lives to worry about. She took Lee by the arm and tried to pull him to his feet. "Lee, I know you're hurt but we've got to go! We've got to make a run for it or we're dead meat!"

Lee rose painfully to his feet, clutched his stomach, and tried to say something to her. But even if he had been strong enough to make himself heard, she was too charged up to hear him. With her heart slamming inside her chest, she wrapped her arm around Lee's waist and the two of them ran up the twisting path that led to the bat cave.

Death was on the trail behind them, grasping a high powered hunting rifle in its sweaty grip. They made it to the first cluster of rocks, but Rebecca knew Lee would never make it the rest of the way up to the bat cave. She slipped her arm from his waist and he slunk to the ground like a sack of potatoes. She put a hand over Lee's mouth to suppress his moans.

She was surprised to note that Lee, although in pain, didn't seem to be bleeding. But she didn't have long to think about it because she could hear the other hunters coming now, crashing through the brush. Then the crashing abruptly stopped.

She whispered in Lee's ear for him to be quiet, then slipped the infrared telescope out of his pants. She put it to her eye and took a look down the incline and into the inky black woods.

She saw a movement and focused in. It was the Frenchman, Bernard. And close behind him was the blonde, Heidi. She looked around some more. No sign of Fletcher or Jorge, at least.

Maybe they were retrieving the bodies of Cara and Brian so the *gifted* Jorge could go to work. She looked to the spot where Melanie had fallen. Heidi was . . . gutting her!

She pulled the telescope away and leaned back against the boulder. She thought she might be sick. And would have been, too, except that she had no time. No time if she wanted to live.

She put the telescope to her eye and looked down the path. Bernard had stopped when he saw the Englishman laying in a grotesque heap with an arrow rammed through his throat and Lee's switchblade still stuck deep in the meat of his thigh.

Chris's face was covered with a bubbly froth of blood. Bernard was hunched down now, looking up the path, suspecting an ambush. Seeing none, he dashed over to where the Englishman lay.

Except he didn't quite make it.

He tripped the wire and the Jivaro Catapult was sprung. Long rusty nails slammed into Bernard with such vicious force it picked him off his feet and crushed him against the tree. Rebecca lost the picture at this point because her hand was trembling too much to focus the telescope.

Well, Rebecca thought with a gruesome whimsy, swallowing hard, Bernard got his wish—to see a Jivaro Catapult close up!

But she didn't have time to gloat. She pulled Lee to his feet, and they started to climb the rocky path to the cave. Back in the woods she could her Heidi screaming—she probably found Bernard and Chris. Now Rebecca had a feeling Heidi wasn't going to be quite as anxious as Bernard to come up that path.

Rebecca wrapped her arm around Lee again and they stumbled up the path to the cave. They collapsed inside the entrance and lay together on the cool surface of the cave floor for an eternal moment, gasping for breath. Then Rebecca forced herself to her feet and trained the telescope down the rocky path.

They hadn't been followed. Not yet, anyway. She looked,

further down the path. Heidi was dragging Melanie's body away. "Jesus," she muttered, dropping the telescope to the ground.

She went over to Lee and knelt down beside him. Some color had returned to his face and he seemed to be reviving somewhat. He reached into his jungle shirt and pulled out the survival book. The front of the binding had a small round hole in it.

Lee opened the book. The hole continued almost completely through the book, stopping four pages short of the rear binding. At the end of the hole a misshapen bullet rolled out. Lee gave Rebecca a knowing look. "Man . . . I feel like I've been kicked by a mule but at least I'm alive. Thanks to . . ."

"Your trap worked, too," Rebecca said. "It got that guy Bernard. The Frenchman."

Lee's eyes gleamed with a strange light. "Did you get the gun?"

"What gun?"

"I tried to tell you back there to get four eyes' gun. And my knives."

"Oh, no," Rebecca moaned, banging her forehead with the palm of her hand. In her panic she had run off and left them.

Lee tried to hide his disappointment, but his despair was evident as he rose to his feet. "Don't worry about it; we still have *this*." He held the book up and the last four pages, the pages the bullet had failed to punch a hole through, fell out.

Lee picked up the first page and shown a beam of light on it. Rebecca looked over his shoulder and read along with him. The trap they were looking at was called a Hotfoot. It consisted of burying a shotgun shell in shallow dirt with the sharp end of a nail resting against the firing cap. The blunted end protruded slightly above ground. When someone stepped on it they got a hotfoot, and then some. It was as simple as that.

Lee stuffed the book back into his pants pocket and picked up the infrared telescope that Rebecca had dropped and looked down the path. He scanned the area for several minutes before saying, "I don't see anyone down there. At least no one alive—wait! Off in the distance . . . looks like someone dragging something down a ravine."

Rebecca hesitated, swallowed hard and said, "They . . . they got Melanie."

She watched Lee's body go tense. He stood motionless with his eye to the telescope for the longest moment, and when he pulled the telescope away, Rebecca saw that a tear had formed there, and was now running down his cheek.

He quickly wiped it away. "Well . . . the ranks are thinning," he said.

But the bad guys were still ahead, Rebecca knew, three to two. Even more if the helicopter pilot returned. Lee seemed determined to even the odds. He removed the gun belts strung about his chest and Rebecca knew he was thinking the same thing she was.

Lee's torn shirt fell open and she saw a nasty black and blue welting forming on his hard pectorals. Lee didn't bother trying to button his ragged shirt. Instead, he reached down to the cave floor for a handful of grime and daubed out the sheen of his body and his face. Then he ran out of the cave and back down the path.

Rebecca started to dig holes into the cave floor. Small holes scattered all about. By the time Lee returned, she had a hole dug for every shotgun shell in the gun belt.

"Whoever dragged away that body—Heidi, I guess—took the gun and hunting knife with her," Lee said. "She left this." Lee flicked open the switchblade and Rebecca could see that the point of the blade had snapped off "It must've broke when it hit that guy's thigh bone. I felt it hit something solid just before I passed out."

"Yeah, it was Heidi who dragged Melanie's body and the weapons away," Rebecca said. "The big, arrogant-looking blond woman."

"Well, lucky for us she also left this." Lee dropped the spiked plank on the ground as he took a moment to catch his breath.

Rebecca started to bang the nails out of the plank with the blunt edge of the hunting knife handle. There were about half as many nails as gunshot shells. Lee noticed the holes and grinned at Rebecca. "Maybe we can snap some of those nails in half; they're pretty rusty. If Fletcher or one of the others step on only one, it may still be enough to get the job done."

They snapped what nails they could and laid out the *hotfoots* like a mini-minefield across a stretch of ground from the entrance of the cave to where they were. Then, exhausted from The Killing Game and the night of terror, they laid down on the cave floor using what was left of Lee's shirt as a pillow and held each other tight.

Lee's nearly naked and bruised body shivered in Rebecca's arms. She kissed his welt and he kissed the bruise alongside her temple where the barrel of the Englishman's gun had caught her. They did what they could to keep each other warm. "Are you going to be all right?" she asked, before moving her kisses to his lips.

"Yeah. My body feels like a big toothache, but I think I'll live," he said. He was quiet for a moment. "I figure they'll wait until morning before they try to bag us. They'll probably figure we're holed up here and they'll be right—except we'll have gone out the back door before they get here."

"You mean . . ."

"Yeah," Lee said. "I'd rather face those bats again than

Fletcher's Weatherby. Any day." Lee looked into the inky blackness beyond the cave. "Or night."

He shivered, either from the chill in the night or fear in his heart, and Rebecca held him tighter.

Twenty-seven

They slept a surprisingly peaceful sleep in each other's arms, and awoke together at dawn.

Dawn was when Fletcher arose.

The cave was dim and pleasantly cool. Outside, the air was already growing hot beneath the red ball of the sun that rose steadily above the horizon line.

"We'd better go," Lee said. "Before Fletcher and the gang get here." He motioned to the crawl hole that led into the bat cave. "When we get in there we'll just hug the wall and make our way over to the tunnel door. Keep the flashlights off and try not to make any noise."

Rebecca nodded. They climbed through the hole and into the bat cave. They ran their hands along the side of the wall and made their way over to the wooden door that opened into the tunnel shaft. They shuddered at every tiny flutter of wings. They were up there, Rebecca knew, hanging upside down until it was time to go out and kill again.

She wondered what blood they drank on this evil and eerie island and figured, like Fletcher and the rest of the hunters, they probably drank the blood of wild pigs.

The door creaked open on the first try. It was easier this time, perhaps because they had opened it the day before. Even so, that unfamiliar sound disturbed the furry, winged beasts. With piercing shrieks, small dark shadows started to drop from the roof of the cave.

Lee rushed to close the door again, and that's when they heard the muffled explosion that came from somewhere near the cave entrance. Someone had gotten a hotfoot. But Rebecca's elation at a trap successfully sprung was short-lived as the bat cave came alive with flying predators. At least they had closed the door again.

Lee flicked on his flashlight and Rebecca could see he was grinning. "I think we got one," he said.

"Yeah," Rebecca said, a little breathless.

"It was either Heidi or Jorge," Lee said. "Fletcher's too smart to fall for that one. Especially if he found Paolo with his gun belt missing. He'd send one of the others in ahead of him."

"So what should we do now?"

"We'll make our way to Jorge's room. And if he's there . . ." Lee ran his finger across his throat as if slitting it. "And then there was one."

They hurried down the twisting tunnel, twin beams of light from their flashlights leading the way. When they neared the door that lead out of the tunnel and into Jorge's room, they paused. A crack of light bled beneath the closed door.

They put their ears to the door but heard nothing. They put their shoulders to the door and pushed it open only a crack and got ready to run back to the tunnel at the slightest sound from inside the room. They still heard nothing, so Lee pushed the door open all the way.

Rebecca screamed, and Lee quickly put his hand over her mouth to muffle the sound. Rebecca composed herself and took in the grisly sight in front of her.

Jorge had been there all right, working throughout the night from the looks of it. Before them on the work table sat two rows of decapitated heads. In the first row were the heads of Kevin, Cara, Brian, and Melanie. In the second row were the heads of Peter, Jan, Paolo, Chris, and Bernard. The eyes had been gouged out of all the heads; one of the eye sockets on Jan's shrunken head was slightly misshapen, compliments of Lee and the crossbow.

Kevin's expression was peaceful—he had been sleeping when he was killed, but Melanie's lips were pulled back in a gruesome smile as if she had been in terrible pain when she died. Cara and Brian's heads seemed to lean against each other on the table. Rebecca felt tears stinging her eyes and her body convulsed with sobs.

Lee angrily swept the heads off the work table with a swoop of his muscular arm. He kicked them all under Jorge's cot, and sank into a wooden chair next to the work table. He dropped his head into his hands.

For the first time since The Killing Game had begun, Rebecca feared Lee might be on the verge of cracking. She choked back her own tears and revulsion and placed reassuring hands on Lee's broad shoulders. "We're going to make it," she said, giving his shoulders a squeeze and the rest of him a strong hug. "We're going to win this damn game!"

Lee looked back at her, and placed his own bloodied bandaged hand on top of her hand. Rebecca hoped her encouragement would give him renewed strength, and when she saw that familiar dark, unquenchable fire flickering in his eyes, she knew she had been successful.

Lee placed his wounded paws on the Plexiglas top of the work table, and fueled by sudden recognition, he pulled the three remaining pages of the survival book out of his back pocket. The top sheet described a trap called the *Head Chopper*.

The trap was a piece of sheet metal on a line, set to swing across an entrance when the door was opened. "We don't have any sheet metal, but I bet this will do." He said, running his hands over the sheet of Plexiglas.

Using the flat end of his knife's blade, where the point

had snapped off, he unscrewed the bolts that held the Plexiglas in place and then removed the Plexiglas from the table top. They found a long coil of rawhide, the type used to sew dead lips and leathery skin together, and strung up the sheet of Plexiglas above the door.

"Stand there for a moment," Lee said to Rebecca, indicating the door frame. Lee slowly swung the lethal sheet of heavy plastic down, stopping the makeshift guillotine blade just short of her neck. "How tall do you think Jorge is?"

"I would guess about three or four inches taller than me," Rebecca said. Lee raised the level of the blade three or four inches, made the necessary adjustments with the rawhide cords, and pulled the instrument of death back.

They set the trigger and ran it to the trip wire. They had no sooner finished when they heard footsteps coming up to the door. They scampered behind the door, leaving it open a crack, and waited.

The door opened and from their vantage point they were able to see Jorge standing in the doorway, his patched eye toward them. In his hand he held a sharp machete. A sharp *bloody* machete. It didn't take a stretch of the imagination to know how it had gotten that way. The answers lay beneath Jorge's cot.

Jorge had seen the work table and realized his little prizes were no longer there. In another moment he would realize that the Plexiglas top was no longer there, either. Suddenly Lee swung the door open. "Hey, geek!" he shouted.

Jorge turned and saw them. Forgetting his caution, he charged into the room with the machete blade held high. The bright light of revenge burned deeply in his eyes. He ran at them, letting out an ungodly yelp that stirred something cold in the pit of Rebecca's stomach.

Jorge didn't get very far. He didn't even know what hit him. Which in a way Rebecca regretted. She would've liked to have seen the fear in his eyes the moment he realized he was facing his last moment on earth. Instead, she would have to settle for watching his head roll across the floor of the tiny room like a runaway bowling ball. She followed its path to where it stopped at Lee's feet.

He kicked it under the cot with the rest of the heads.

"Now what?" Rebecca asked.

As usual, the answer was found on the remaining pages of the survival book. Lee flattened the next sheet out on the table top and they read it together. The next trap was a helicopter trap. It consisted of running a long length of wire from a tree top to a center of a clearing where the helicopter would probably land. The wire itself didn't bring the chopper down, but when the wire snapped, it wrapped itself around the chopper's rotor head and caused the pilot to lose control.

"Where do we get that much wire?" Rebecca asked.

"My guess is in a supply shed. Or someplace like that."

"I haven't seen any near the house, have you?" Rebecca asked.

"No, and I haven't seen any electrical wires running away from the house, either. Fletcher must have some kind of generator pumping the juice. Either run by a battery or by gas. I think if we can find that we'll have everything else we need."

"You mean . . . you want to go back to the house?"

Lee nodded. "If Heidi stepped on a hotfoot back there, Fletcher'll probably return to the house to call for the chopper. With any luck we may be able to beat him there and kill two birds with one stone."

Lee pried the machete loose from the hand of Jorge's headless corpse. Then they peered outside the little cabin that leaned into the cliff wall. It looked clear and Rebecca dashed out the door followed closely by Lee, who grasped the machete in his unbandaged hand. They took the path that led down to the beach. Even though the beach provided no cover, they wanted to get to Fletcher's house before he did and every second counted.

They reached the lagoon safely and climbed the rocks to the top of the cliff. From there, they made their way to the hunting lodge. They peered inside the window and saw no sign of life. They listened carefully, not daring to breathe, and were rewarded when they heard a barely perceptible, soft humming sound. "It's the generator," Lee said. "It must be in the basement."

They circled the house, staying low, until they came across the cellar door. It was heavily padlocked. Lee looked at Rebecca. She knew what she had to do. She removed the skeleton key from her neck and moments later they were in the basement.

It was a gas-run generator, and a row of fifty gallon gasoline cans were lined up against the wall. Next to the gas was a large locker. They threw the locker doors open and found it stuffed with supplies. "Bingo!" Lee exclaimed happily.

Lee grabbed a long coil of wire and a long metal bolt and the two of them ran back to the clearing. Lee climbed the tallest pine tree he could find while Rebecca kept a look out. He tied the wire to the highest tree branch and dropped the coil to the ground where Rebecca retrieved it.

Rebecca took the coil and ran to the center of the clearing, unraveling the coil as she went. She felt terribly vulnerable in the center of the clearing. A sitting duck. Her hands were trembling as she tied the loose end of the wire to the bolt, expecting at any moment for a bullet to come crashing into her.

She hammered the bolt deep into the muddy ground until the top of the bolt was entirely submerged. She piled on even more mud to completely hide the bolt and then ran out of there. She reached the cover of the brush at the same time Lee was dropping out of the pine tree.

It wasn't a moment too soon. The unmistakable sound of the chopper's whooping blade cut through the still, early morning air. The dot on the horizon grew louder as it grew closer. From their vantage point in the brush, they saw Fletcher and Heidi appear at the edge of the clearing and look up into the sky.

Fletcher had the Weatherby. He and Heidi were both limping. Fletcher from his bad leg, and Heidi because what was left of her right foot was wrapped in a dirty, bloody gauze that was unraveling quickly as the two hunters made their way to where the descending helicopter was swooping down into the clearing.

Rebecca held her breath, and she felt Lee take her hand in his.

The wire snapped with a twang and wrapped itself around the rotor head. The machine veered to the left and then to the right as the pilot tried to regain control of his aircraft.

Fletcher stopped dead in his tracks as Heidi continued to run toward the tottering chopper. Either he had suspected the possibility of a trap, or it was just sheer instinct, but even before the chopper hit the ground, Fletcher turned back toward the house.

And then the chopper was plummeting to the ground.

Twenty-eight

The chopper came down right on top of Heidi. The effect was dramatic. Heidi, the chopper, and anyone in it went up in a red ball of fire.

Rebecca and Lee held up their hands as a wave of heat blew their way. And then they hit the ground as another explosion ripped through the air. When the ground finally stopped vibrating they scrambled to their feet. They were in time to see Fletcher, half his face bloodied, limping quickly toward the house, still clutching the Weatherby.

The door to the hunting lodge slammed shut and locked as she and Lee reached the edge of the clearing.

"I guess Fletcher went in the house for a little cold cream," Lee said with a bitter smile.

Rebecca reached up to remove the pendant that held the skeleton key. Fletcher could run, but he couldn't hide. Not behind a locked door on this nightmare of an island, at any rate. They would finish the game.

But Lee reached out to stop her. "This one's on me."

He pulled the survival book out of his back pocket and took out that last, loose page. The trap was called *The Flaming Gas Trap*. And it was the simplest and most cruelly effective of all the traps.

The instructions were simple: Pour a can of gas down someone's chimney and then sit back and wait for the fireworks to begin.

They jogged back to the house and down into the cellar where Lee removed a fifty gallon can of gas from the row that ran along the wall next to the generator. Then he took a book of kitchen matches from the supply locker as Rebecca picked up a ladder that rested next to a row of paint cans.

They went back outside and Rebecca leaned the ladder against the side of the house. She held it as Lee climbed up, muscles bulging as he lugged the heavy can of gas with him. They were working as a team. Cool and efficient. A killing machine so finely honed—their thoughts could be interchangeable.

And why wouldn't they be?

They had been well-trained by the master.

While Lee was making his way up the slippery shingles to the chimney, Rebecca went around the front of the house and found a clump of bushes ten or fifteen feet from the front door. She ran trip wire across the path and tied it securely to a bush. The trip wire glistened in the sunlight. If Fletcher came running out that front door he might be looking for a trip wire and see it just in time. Rebecca let the line go slack and carefully covered it with leaves.

She'd trip this one herself.

She stepped away from the house and looked up to the roof. Lee was at the chimney and waiting. He gave her a little wave. She waved back and he poured the entire fifty gallon can of gasoline down the chimney. He yanked what was left of the survival book from his back pocket. He gave it a good long look, as if it were a friend he was sad to see go, then he kissed it and set it on fire with a kitchen match he lit with his thumbnail.

He threw the flaming book down the chimney.

The size of the explosion surprised both of them. She noticed Lee's startled expression as the roof buckled beneath his feet. Then he was sliding down the other side of the house and out of sight. A chunk of shingle came cartwheeling out of nowhere and grazed the top of Rebecca's head, knocking her backward.

She sat up, stunned. A flow of blood from a scalp wound found its way into her eyes and she frantically wiped it away with the back of her hand.

Then the door to the hunting lodge banged open.

Fletcher came running out of the house faster than Rebecca thought any man with a limp could possibly go, so fast he almost ran right past her. He wasn't using the Weatherby for a cane now—he held the big gun in front of him cocked and ready to fire.

She groped for the wire, desperately wiping away the blood with the sleeve of her camouflage shirt.

Fletcher must've heard her or seen her or sensed she was there because even as he ran, he was leveling the Weatherby right at her.

She yanked the wire taut and Fletcher went down as if he'd had his legs kicked right out from under him. He flew through the air with a surprised expression on his face, losing his grip on the big hunting rifle. The Weatherby spun around and struck the ground hard, butt first. Then it roared and barked out a long tongue of flame.

Fletcher's surprised expression was blown clean off his face.

Then the rest of his head came apart in wet, glittering fragments.

Lee was right about that Weatherby, Rebecca thought. It really packed a wallop.

When the smoke cleared, Rebecca walked over to the thing on the ground that used to be Fletcher and looked down. That's one head no one's going to shrink, she thought.

She tore off a patch of Fletcher's safari jacket and dabbed at the cut on her head.

THE KILLING GAME

Then she hurried around to the far side of the house to find Lee. She found him lying on the ground about thirty yards away from the pyre that used to be the hunting lodge. He must've staggered and fallen. She rushed to his side in time to see his eyes flickering as if trying to reignite his bruised brainwaves.

"Are you all right?" She had lost count of how many times she had asked him that question.

Lee's eyes slowly came into focus. "Yeah," he muttered. "Just all them things that used to hurt are hurting a little more right now." He paused, then said, "I hope you got him. Because I'm not in the mood to go hunting right now."

"I got him."

Lee smiled in spite of the pain. Then he saw the blood. "What happened . . ."

He tried to get up but she waved him down. He was still too dazed to be on his feet and she was feeling pretty dizzy herself. She lay on the ground next to him and together they watched Fletcher's house burn as nonchalantly as if they were watching a campfire.

Lee wiped away a trickle of blood that was making its way down Rebecca's forehead. "Are you sure you're all right?"

They had made it. They had won The Killing Game. And by winning The Killing Game, Rebecca had found the boy she thought she could live with for the rest of her life. She leaned over and kissed him, blood and all.

"Oh . . . I'll survive," she said.

Twenty-nine

Rebecca and Lee walked into the Night Owl Club, hand in hand. Rebecca looked around for familiar faces and found none. She was determined to put her sadness behind her and have a good time this evening, their first night back in Cooper Hollow.

"Yo, Lee," yelled a deep voice. "Hey, bro, over here."

Rebecca turned in the direction of the shout and recognized the tough guys in a back booth, the ones who had given her and Lee a ride from the country club. That day seemed like a lifetime ago.

"Some other time," Lee called toward the booth and led Rebecca toward the bar where Jenny was wiping up a spilled soda.

"Hi, Jenny," Rebecca said cheerfully.

"Hi, Rebecca. Lee." Jenny stopped her work for a moment and smiled at them. Her violet eyes shone in the dark club.

Rebecca wanted to tell Jenny all about what had happened on the island, about how Jenny's presents had saved their lives. About how she was right—there *were* ghosts on the island, benevolent spirits that helped them use Jenny's gifts to fight and destroy Fletcher and his evil hunters. But Jenny's smile seemed to say, "I know what happened and I'm glad you're both back safe." Rebecca said nothing.

"So, what'll it be?" Jenny asked, breaking the silence.

"I'll have a cherry coke," Lee said.

THE KILLING GAME

"Me, too," Rebecca added.

"Coming right up," Jenny said as she walked down to the other end of the bar to get their drinks.

Rebecca fingered the pendant that still hung around her neck. *Thanks, Jenny* she said silently.

"You're welcome," Jenny answered from the other end of the bar.

"What did she say?" asked Lee perplexed.

"Oh, nothing." Rebecca turned back to Lee and kissed him full on the mouth. They were still kissing when Jenny brought them their sodas.

THE NIGHT OWL CLUB
IT'S COOL—
IT'S FUN—
IT'S TERRIFYING—
AND YOU CAN JOIN IT ... IF YOU DARE!

THE NIGHTMARE CLUB #1: JOY RIDE (4315, $3.50)
by Richard Lee Byers

All of Mike's friends know he has a problem—he doesn't see anything wrong with drinking and driving. But then a pretty new girl named Joy comes to The Night Owl Club, and she doesn't mind if he drinks and drives. In fact, she encourages it. And what Mike doesn't know might kill him because Joy is going to take him on the ride of his life!

THE NIGHTMARE CLUB #2: THE INITIATION (4316, $3.50)
by Nick Baron

Kimberly will do anything to join the hottest clique at her school. And when her boyfriend, Griff, objects to her new "bad" image, Kimberly decides that he is a wimp. Then kids start drowning in a nearby lake—and she starts having nightmares about an evil water spirit that has a hold over her new friends. Kimberly knows that she must resist the monster's horrible demands in order to save Griff and the other kids' lives—and her very soul!

THE NIGHTMARE CLUB #3: WARLOCK GAMES (4317, $3.50)
by Richard Lee Byers

Mark, the newest cadet at Hudson Military Academy, is falling for Laurie, a student at rival school, Cooper High. So, he does not want to be involved in the feud between the two schools. But fellow cadet, Greg Tobias, persuades Mark to join other cadets in playing weird and violent pranks on Cooper High. Then Mark discovers that Greg is a centuries-old warlock who is playing a deadly game of chess with a fellow demon in which the students are the pawns—and now Mark must break Greg's deadly hold or they will all become victims of a terrifying evil ...

THE NIGHTMARE CLUB #4: THE MASK (4349, $3.50)
by Nick Baron

While looking for a costume for the Nightmare Club's Halloween party, average-looking Sheila finds a weird mask in a local antique barn. When she puts it on, she turns into a real knockout, and soon is getting lots of attention. Then good-looking kids start dying and Sheila realizes the truth. When she wears the mask, its guardian spirit gets stronger. And unless Sheila can resist its seductive magic she will become a prisoner of its murderous evil forever!

Available wherever paperbacks are sold, or order direct from the Publisher. Send cover price plus 50¢ per copy for mailing and handling to Penguin USA, P.O. Box 999, c/o Dept. 17109, Bergenfield, NJ 07621. Residents of New York and Tennessee must include sales tax. DO NOT SEND CASH.

LIGHTS ... CAMERA ... ACTION!

VIDEO HIGH
by Marilyn Kaye

Meet Sharon Delaney, Tyler Ratcliff, Debra Lewis, Jade Barrow, Zack Stevenson, and Kris Hogan. They're all students at Greenwood High ... and the cast of the hottest new show on cable TV.

Share the experiences of six high school students who set up their own cable TV show, which deals with the issues, concerns, and problems of teens today.

VIDEO HIGH #1: MODERN LOVE (4483, $3.50)

VIDEO HIGH #2: THE HIGH LIFE (4545, $3.50)

VIDEO HIGH #3:
DATE IS A FOUR-LETTER WORD (4610, $3.50)

VIDEO HIGH #4: THE BODY BEAUTIFUL (4674, $3.50)

VIDEO HIGH #5:
THE COLORS OF THE HEART (4733, $3.50)

Available wherever paperbacks are sold, or order direct from the Publisher. Send cover price plus 50¢ per copy for mailing and handling to Penguin USA, P.O. Box 999, c/o Dept. 17109, Bergenfield, NJ 07621. Residents of New York and Tennessee must include sales tax. DO NOT SEND CASH.

THE *VOICE* OF LIFE AND LOVE IN THE '90s.

A VOICES ROMANCE #1: SECOND TO NONE (4514, $3.50)
by ArLynn Presser
Seventeen-year-old Garnet Brown has learned to cope with an absentee father. But right now she's just concerned with getting into a good college so she can leave the old neighborhood behind. Then Garnet's father comes back into her life and things start unraveling. And only Grant, her sensitive, intelligent tutor can help Garnet see the truth beyond appearances.

**A VOICES ROMANCE #2:
DIFFERENT RAINBOWS** (4580, $3.50)
by Judith Daniels
Sierra Costa is tired of being teased by her classmates who say she is the daughter of "hippies", so she rebels by taking on a conservative lifestyle and boyfriend. But after surprising results, she learns to start accepting herself *and* the people she loves for who and what they are.

A VOICES ROMANCE #3: STARRING MOM (4642, $3.50)
by Mallory Tarcher
When Dena was five years old, her mother left to "find herself". Now at sixteen, Dena has been reunited with her newly famous mother. All this time Dena has been searching for the *perfect* mother. But by accepting her mom for who she is, Dena finds that she already has her very own version of a fantastic mom!

A VOICES ROMANCE #4: THE ROMANTICS (4705, $3.50)
by ArLynn Presser
Sixteen-year-old Ursula has spent her entire life moving around. Now a senior, her family has settled and Ursula will do anything to be part of the in-crowd. Then she meets Eastman Hawke, a guy who doesn't fit in—and doesn't want to.

Available wherever paperbacks are sold, or order direct from the Publisher. Send cover price plus 50¢ per copy for mailing and handling to Penguin USA, P.O. Box 999, c/o Dept. 17109, Bergenfield, NJ 07621. Residents of New York and Tennessee must include sales tax. DO NOT SEND CASH.